About the Author:

Juliana Hutchings has had horses all her life, and her wonderful experiences as a rider, trainer, and instructor inspired her to write *A Horse to Remember*, her first novel, at age fourteen. A junior in high school, she lives with her family in Landenberg, Pennsylvania where she manages a horse farm and competes at the preliminary level in eventing. Look for more books from her in the future.

To my readers,

I hope you enjoy this story of love and respect as much as I enjoyed telling it. Determination and persistence can transform any vision into reality. Never abandon your dreams.

Juliana Hutchings

A Horse to Remember

by

Julianna Hutchings

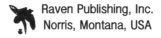
Raven Publishing, Inc.
Norris, Montana, USA

Published by: Raven Publishing, Inc., PO Box 2866
Norris, MT 59745

Copyright © 2007 by Juliana Hutchings
Cover and inside photographs © 2007 by Isabelle Hutchings
A Horse to Remember
ISBN: 0-9772525-1-5
Printed in the United States

Library of Congress Cataloging-in-Publication Data
Hutchings, Juliana, 1989-
A horse to remember / by Juliana Hutchings.
    p. cm.
Summary: When Hilary's family moves from Delaware to a small
town in Tennessee, she forms a connection with a wild stallion that
seems as lonely and out of place as herself and decides to secretly train
him to save him from the slaughterhouse.
    ISBN 0-9772525-1-5 (pbk.)
    1. Youths' writings, American. [1. Horses--Training- Fiction. 2.
Mustang--Fiction. 3. Wild horses--Fiction. 4. Self-esteem--Fiction. 5.
Moving, Household--Fiction. 6. Tennessee--Fiction. 7. Youths' writ-
ings.] I. Title.
    PZ7.H961617Hor 2007
    [Fic]--dc22
                                                    2006027552

Dedicated to my loving cat, Sing-Sing,
who warmed my lap through the
duration of writing this book.
In Loving Memory of Sing-Sing
1991-2004

Hilary's glossary of horse terms
may be found on pages
172-176

.

Chapter One

*H*ilary Thompson gazed out the car's window, straining to see through the pouring rain. While the raindrops rolled down the window, she recalled the unexpected events of the past few weeks.

It all started on Monday almost three weeks ago. She had just returned home from a usual day of school and an afternoon of fun at Ali's house. She found her parents waiting at the door. Her mother looked worried, and Hilary could have sworn the wrinkles on her father's face were more prominent than ever. They ushered her into the kitchen where Sam, her younger brother, sat, looking puzzled.

"We have an important announcement to make," James began, glancing at his wife. "I don't know how to put this but…" he paused and then continued, "we're moving to Tennessee." He had been transferred from the hospital where he'd worked as a surgeon for years to another, far from home. They would all have to move, and Hilary wasn't given any say in the matter.

"We have picked out a beautiful home! You'll love it, Hilary. Just wait and see," Karen assured her daughter.

"There's plenty of space, and you'll never have to fall asleep to the sound of traffic again!" Karen told her it was located in the heart of horse country. Why on earth would Hilary's parents buy a house in horse country? To her it was the same as purchasing a shack in the middle of Alaska. Was there even a respectable school nearby? Hilary needed a civilized place to begin her freshman year of high school.

She had lived in Hockessin, Delaware, where little to nothing ever occurred. With a shopping center next to her house, the noise never ended. There was the constant sound of slamming car doors and trucks racing up and down the busy road. She knew it had not been the ideal place to live, but it was all she'd ever known. Now her whole way of life was changing, and Hilary didn't think it was for the better.

Her friends Ali and Joy were the best things that had ever happened to her. They were always there to cheer her up when she was down, to offer a hand when she needed help, or to laugh with her when she just wanted to have fun. Hilary recalled all the fun things her friends had done for her before she left. Joy had thrown an enormous party with many kids from Thorndale Junior High School. She even invited Chris, Hilary's highschool dream guy. Ali had snapped pictures of everyone, doing everything from the moment the celebration started to the moment it ended. Hilary giggled as she scanned the pictures Ali had given her. One showed her face when she saw Chris arrive, others were of her in the pool, and some were of Ali and Joy, so she wouldn't forget them.

As the car traveled silently along the highway, headed

for Lewisburg, Tennessee, the rain stopped, the sun began to shine, and Hilary's spirits rose. She saw green fields, white board fences, and horses swishing their tails in the shade of large trees. Hilary checked to see if her mother and younger brother were still awake.

"No, of course not," Hilary said to herself, eyeing her fellow travelers. "I'm the only one who can't sleep."

"What was that, darling?" James asked, keeping his eyes fixed on the road ahead.

"Err—nothing, Dad," Hilary responded, glaring at her brother, who was taking up more than his half of the seat. His knotted, sandy-brown hair resembled a rat's nest, and he breathed heavily, like a dog. Hilary felt the urge to give him a push and watch him collapse onto the floor. Karen didn't help the situation, either, for she had the front seat back as far as it would go, digging into Hilary's long, slender legs. She looked relaxed and comfortable, smiling to herself as she slept, which agitated Hilary even more.

"Dad, how much longer until we get there?" Hilary questioned, unbuckling her seat belt and inching toward her father. Before he could answer, there was a huge thump on the floor of the silver Nissan.

"Oops! Sorry, Sammy," Hilary lied, as her brother lay crumpled on the floor.

"Hil, what am I going to do with you? If you don't stop picking on your little brother, there will be consequences," James said. When his eyes met Hilary's in the rearview mirror, he joined in her contagious laughter.

As Hilary and James settled down, an enormous

weight lifted from Hilary's shoulders. Maybe everything would work out. Her new home would be a second chapter in her life, opening unseen doors and inviting new experiences. And maybe she would make new friends who would become just as special to her as Joy and Ali. She doubted it, but you never knew. *You just never knew.*

Chapter Two

*H*ilary fell into a restful sleep and dreamt of her old home with Ali, Joy, and even Chris. But all too soon she heard voices arousing her from her much-needed rest. Sitting up, she realized that the car had stopped; they had arrived at their new home. She watched her parents stride into the house and close the door behind them. Climbing out of the car to stretch her cramped limbs, Hilary decided to take a look around, leaving Sam asleep.

She scrutinized the house, cringing with displeasure. The window shutters were a soft pink and the large entrance door was a violet purple. It resembled a doll house she'd played with when she was five. In the back of the rolling yard was a short row of pines with flowers scattered around them. Flicking her ponytail, she looked south of the property, brightening at what she saw.

Or maybe it was what she heard. Adjacent to her yard was a fence on the edge of a horse farm that seemed to stretch for miles. Buildings, large and small, were scattered across the property, and from inside, horses called to others in the fields. Some of the fences surrounded sand and others grass, but either way, horses were everywhere. There was a deciduous forest to the east of the property spreading as far as she could see, like a pair of eagle's wings, embracing the farm.

The sound of troubled voices drifted from the other side of a building where Hilary could just make out a small truck and trailer. She couldn't understand the words or see the people, so she crept closer and strained to hear more. *Still nothing.* "I've got to get closer," she whispered to herself as though she were a detective solving a troubling mystery. She crossed a small paddock to a cluster of trees. Here Hilary could see where the voices were coming from without being spotted. In the large barnyard, a tall slender woman stood listening as an older woman spoke.

"I just can't deal with him. He is too much of a challenge," she said. "I got him from Robert, who got him from the mustang adoption agency. You know Robert, a real nice guy, but when he realized he couldn't handle this animal, he was going to take him to the slaughterhouse. You know me, Susan, I just couldn't let that happen. So I took him in and found him to be a beast of a horse. Rob said he had ridden him once or twice, but I can't even get near him. I'm not one to go back on my word, but…" she paused and looked around as if to make sure no one was eavesdropping.

Hilary ducked lower into the bushes, relieved that the old lady had not seen her. Then, in an even quieter voice, the woman continued, "Well, the truth is, before you called I was going to take him—you know where. He's just too wild. But anyway, I am so glad you're taking him off my hands. You do have a way with horses. And actually he's not that bad." She chuckled nervously.

"Well, Mary, I will do my best, but if you say he's really a…" Susan began, then turned to look at the bushes where Hilary was hidden. "I can't give you any guarantees, but I'll do my best with him," she said.

"Thank you, and you never know, he may turn out to be a nice horse for your boy," Mary said.

"We'll see," Susan responded.

Hilary wondered what was so bad about the horse they were fussing over. Her question was answered just moments later. The women disappeared inside the trailer and reappeared with a black horse. He was different from any horse Hilary had ever seen. Head high and nostrils flaring, he skidded away from his handlers just as his hind feet reached solid ground.

They tried to calm him but the horse broke away, two lead ropes flying behind him, the women scrambling to catch up. He galloped toward the nearest field. His feet seemed to barely touch the ground, and his tail billowed behind him. The other horses threw their heads up.

Hilary had to see what happened next. She fled from the bushes and ran to where the others had disappeared behind a barn. She saw that Mary and Susan had cornered the black horse near a small vacant pasture.

"Mary, open that gate!" called Susan. Mary scuttled as fast as her stout legs would take her and swung the gate open. The horse bolted in and stood quivering against the fence. The corral Susan had chosen was right in front of

Hilary. She had to get out of there.

Once safely back in her yard, she let out a long sigh of relief, thankful she hadn't been seen. For a girl who knew nothing about horses, she understood one thing—the horse she'd just seen was lonely and out of place, not aggressive and dangerous as Mary had described. She recalled how he'd shot off toward the other horses, as if starved for social interactions. A strange tingle crept up her spine as Hilary realized that she, too, was lonely and out of place in her new surroundings. *She was just like the black horse.*

"Where've you been, Hil?" the sloppy-haired eight-year-old asked as he crawled out of the car.

"Well, actually I just got up, and…and I was looking at the house," Hilary lied. "It could use some repainting." Normally, Hilary had to admit, she was a good fibber. But after what she'd just witnessed, she was uneasy. Sam eyed her suspiciously, then turned and marched off toward the porch.

The two kids ran into the house and searched all the rooms. Sam got to the largest bedroom first and declared it his. Hilary's initial anger was replaced with outright fury when her mother allowed Sam to keep the room. She decided it was best that she stay in her room and unpack her things before she got into an argument with her brother. Hilary arranged her room in a neat, cozy fashion with her bed hugging the wall nearest the window. And then, just when she thought she'd finished moving furniture, her parents asked her to help Sam.

"Why can't you do this yourself, Sam?" asked Hilary,

as she struggled to push his bookshelf to the far corner of the room, "All your stuff goes outside—like your baseballs and soccer balls, so why do you have to have such a big room?" The space was open and airy, much too big for an eight-year-old sports fanatic.

"I need somewhere to practice my karate," Sam replied, smiling matter-of-factly.

Unlike her brother, Hilary didn't have any hobbies. Back in Delaware, she'd always hung out at the mall and thought about boys 24/7. It worried her that she wouldn't have much to do at her new home with no friends or shopping malls. Karen had told her to enroll in a softball or volleyball camp during the summer months, but she had disregarded her mother's advice, choosing to sit around for the vacation and be miserable.

Dinner was quiet in the new home that night. Hilary thought about what had happened earlier and decided she wouldn't even go near her brother and risk getting in another fight with him. Karen was the first to break the silence. She lifted her wine glass and said, "Cheers to our new home." They all clinked their glasses together noisily. As though a spell had been lifted, talking erupted inside the kitchen. Karen and James discussed the new house and how easy the drive down had been. Sam periodically shot questions to his father about the baseball field he wanted to build, and Hilary asked her mother about nearby malls. As dinner slowly came to an end, Karen stood up and began washing the plates in the shiny, new sink.

"Hilary, I'd like to speak with you, so don't go to bed just yet," Karen said. "Your father and I have decided that you should get a job this summer to keep you and your brother from bickering so much."

"We think it would be a good way for you to earn a little extra pocket money. It'll give you something to do," added James.

"Do you have any ideas?" Hilary asked her parents. "I mean, it's not like I'm good at anything."

"Oh, honey, stop that. You know you have many talents. You just need to put them to use," said Karen.

"Okay, so back to my first question—do you have any ideas on what job I should do?" Hilary asked.

"Actually, yes," James began, exchanging a glance with Karen. "We were thinking you could get a job at the stables next door."

"Doing what, Dad, picking up after horses?"

"Well, yeah, honey. And not only that but you'd make some friends, also."

"Did you hear that, Mom? Ha. Come on now. This has got to be a joke. Right? You want me to do something with my *talents,* so you send me to a farm to shovel manure? I'm appalled at you both." Hilary felt sick to her stomach. She looked around the room, deliberately avoiding eye contact with her parents.

As soon as Hilary's head of wavy, auburn hair hit her pillow, her eyes closed, and the sun slipped behind the horizon. She slept until a noise disturbed the silence of the night. Sitting up, she peered out of the window beside her bed and tried to focus her eyes on the farm next door. What she saw made her eyes open so wide she felt they might pop out. The black horse she'd seen yesterday was galloping frantically around the small paddock near her house. In the light of the moon he shimmered with sweat; his head was held high in the air.

"He's completely lost his mind!" Hilary muttered, pressing her nose to the glass for a better look. The frightened animal began to speed up, moving faster and faster. Then, without any warning, he charged toward the fence and soared over it with inches to spare. After landing safely, the horse tore off toward the road, showing no signs of stopping. Hilary knew she had to do something. She couldn't let him get hit by a car, even if he was a lunatic horse. She lurched out of bed, threw on her slippers, and hurtled down the twisty steps, baggy pajama pants billowing. Suddenly she stopped dead in her tracks.

Chapter Three

"Umm...hi, Dad," Hilary croaked, gawking at her father in the kitchen.

"Well, hello, honey. What brings you down at two-thirty in the morning? You seem to be in quite a rush," James said as he sipped a cup of tea.

"Well, I'm not the only one up. What are *you* doing awake?" Hilary asked, taking a seat on the stool next to her father's.

"Oh no you don't, young lady. I asked you first."

"I was thirsty and needed to get a drink. So I came running down here because...well, I was thirsty, Dad." Hilary answered, spinning off the stool and heading back up the stairs. "Wait a sec. You didn't tell me why you were up, now did you? And why are you all dressed in your scrubs?"

"Hilary, you know exactly why. My new shift in the hospital starts at four. I thought I'd get an early start, take a shower, and eat," James told his daughter. "Now you'd better get some sleep, or you'll be awfully crabby when your mother gets you up."

"What do you mean, gets me up?" Hilary asked, cocking her head and slinking back to her father.

"I mean, Hilary, that your mother scheduled an appointment for you at eight. She's taking you to the farm next door for a job interview. Won't that be fun?"

"Ughhh!" was all Hilary managed, proud of herself for not spurting out the rest of her thoughts. Forgetting all about the black horse and about getting a drink, she marched up the stairs and crawled into bed, and although she was furious, tried to get some sleep.

She awoke the next morning to the pleasant chirping of the birds. It was so different from the constant hum of cars, that Hilary hardly minded her mother's incessant nagging to get dressed.

"All right, all right already, I'll get up," Hilary called, thinking back to mornings at her old home. They seemed so far off, as though trapped in a dreamland that didn't exist. On weekends she would sleep until twelve or so, then hit the mall with her friends. They spent hours talking about guys and laughing over past events. In the evening they would hang out at Ali's because her mom never minded their company.

"Okay, come get breakfast, Hil," Karen called, stirring Hilary from her recollections. As Hilary pulled on some jeans and hurried down to the kitchen, her mind drifted back to the black horse. She wondered if he was far gone by now, maybe out west in some wild horse herd; she wondered if he was even still alive.

Now head on into the barn. Susan Collins said she'll be waiting," said Karen, pulling into the farm entrance. "I don't have time to walk you in, because I'm taking your brother to the park, and then I have an appointment with the school and…"

"Mom, I get the picture. I'll be fine, okay?"

Karen nodded and followed the circle around the barn parking lot as she drove away.

Hilary walked uncertainly into the nearest large green barn. Above the entrance was a beautifully crafted wooden sign that read:

MILLBROOKE STABLES

Inside, horses of every color poked their heads over the stall doors where a chart, listing the resident horse's name, breeding, owner, and description, hung. People were everywhere. Some were feeding, and others were getting water from the spigot outside. Kids led horses to and from the barn, and others had horses tied in the aisle. It was the same outdoors in the arenas. The ring closest to the barn was being used for what Hilary guessed was a lesson. Another ring had a brown horse going around on a rope. She looked out at a large open field bordering the woods and saw more kids riding over jumps.

"Would you move please? You're kind of in our way," spoke an icy voice.

Hilary turned to see a blonde-haired girl, probably her

own age, leading a horse with dapples. The girl was very pretty, with long legs like Hilary's and beautiful blue eyes, which didn't match her smug expression. She was dressed in clean white riding breeches with shiny black boots. There was an air about her that warned Hilary to keep her distance. Just to be friendly, she said, "That's a nice horse you have there. Is he yours?"

"Actually, he's a she, and I know she's nice. Lady is the top jumper on the farm, besides Susan's horse, Lotto, that is. What are you doing here anyway? I know all of the faces at this barn, being I'm the top student, and you sure don't ring any bells." The girl smirked, eyeing Hilary up and down.

"Well, I was kind of looking for Susan, or whoever runs the stable. Do you know where I might find her?"

"Yes, it's Susan," answered the girl as she and Lady stepped past Hilary. "And my name is Elise, by the way," she called back as she disappeared around the corner.

Hilary was confused and angry. How could Elise be so rude? But then a comforting hand rested on her shoulder, easing her angry thoughts.

"You must be Hilary. I'm Susan," said a friendly voice. Hilary pivoted to face the speaker. As she suspected, it was the same lady she'd seen yesterday. Hilary smiled and nodded, unsure of what to say.

"Come in here and we can talk." Susan gestured to a door to the right of the aisle. "This is my office. It's where I keep track of all my riding students and their paperwork," she said, opening the door and following Hilary inside.

Photos big and small lined the walls. Above them, a wire stretched across the room with ribbons dangling from it. In the corner, trophies of various shapes and sizes fought for space on the shelves. Hilary took a seat in front of Susan's desk and commented nervously on how beautiful the farm was.

"Thank you. It is a wonderful place, and I am blessed to live here. It's the perfect facility for teaching lessons and training horses. So tell me, Hilary, have you had any experience with horses?"

Hilary hesitated, choosing her words carefully. Even if she didn't want the job, she couldn't make a complete fool of herself. "Not exactly; I've ridden horses at fairs and stuff but nothing more. And I've never really worked around them either—or even at a farm." Hilary finished, gazing uncertainly into Susan's kind face.

"Well, everyone has to start somewhere, right? I began riding when I was very young, but I still remember learning all the dos and don'ts about horses. And, even today, after all these years, I'm still learning. Do you have any hobbies?"

Hilary cringed. "No, not really. I kind of wish I did, though."

"Well, your mom told me you just moved here yesterday, so I surely don't expect you to find something you love just yet. Now, down to business. I understand you want a summer job working on the farm, is that correct?" Susan asked, smiling encouragingly as she leaned back in her chair.

"Yes," Hilary lied, wishing her mother had never gotten her into this mess.

"Terrific. Here is a list of what you will do each day. Go ahead and take a look at it, so you can ask me any questions you might have now. I am due in the ring in about three minutes," she finished, consulting her watch. Hilary read the list:

Jobs

1. Clean out my four horses' stalls.
2. Clean out stalls of the boarders who signed up on the list on the barn notice board.
3. Water and hay my horses for the day while they are in their stalls.
4. Sweep the barn aisles.
5. Groom my horses.
6. Feel free to get lunch and drinks in the lounge.

It all seemed so easy to Hilary. She thought she must have read the list wrong, so she re-read it until she realized she must look like the slowest reader in the world. "Is this all I have to do, Ms. Collins? It just looks so simple," she asked, looking up.

"That's it, Hilary. It looks simple. Believe me a lot of my boarders—" She paused, realizing Hilary wasn't familiar with this term, "people who pay to keep their horses here—don't come out each day. They sign up on the list for someone else to clean their stall. Normally, my students do the cleaning for extra riding lessons, but now it's all on you. Since I have to go, I'll have my son, Jeremy give you a tour of the place and explain the list further."

"Okay," said Hilary, following the sandy-haired woman to the smaller barn.

"Jeremy will be in there somewhere," Susan said.

But he wasn't. Hilary looked in every stall, then headed to the other barn, but still couldn't find him. She was just about to give up when an ear-piercing squeal came from the small paddock by her house. She saw a boy get up from the ground and dust off his pants.

"Are you okay?" called Hilary as she ran to him. She couldn't help but notice how cute he was with his dusty-brown hair and lean, athletic figure.

"Yeah, I'm good as ever." He smiled, checking Hilary out as well, apparently not the slightest bit embarrassed. "So who are you? Haven't seen you around here before."

"I'm…" Hilary began but Jeremy interrupted.

"No, no, let me guess. You just moved into the old Turner place," Jeremy said as though he weren't asking a question. "I saw the moving trucks in there on Wednesday. You've got some nice furniture." Hilary blushed. She didn't know what to say. She was normally so casual with guys, but for some unknown reason, she was tense with this one. He was good-looking, but Hilary had interacted with plenty of cute guys before.

"Yeah, I guess we do." After it came out, she realized how stupid she must sound—she shouldn't have said anything. Then something else caught her attention. Something black moved in the corner of the small paddock.

Hilary couldn't distinguish what it was since the large oak tree from her yard shaded the corral.

"What's in this pen?" she asked tapping the fence and squinting some more at the corner. Then she saw him. The black horse stepped out of the shade and snorted.

Chapter Four

"You don't want to know," Jeremy said as he climbed up and sat on the fence once more. "I was sitting like this a minute ago, and Satan charged over and scared me half to death."

"But...how did..." Hilary began, confused at what she had seen. If the horse escaped last night, then how did anyone ever catch him? Or did he just return to the paddock himself? Only one way to find out. "Well, I thought I saw that horse jump the fence last night and, well, I'm wondering how he got back in?" Hilary asked, looking into the boy's dark brown eyes.

"He never jumped the fence. You must have been dreaming. Well, I have to run, but I'll see you around, okay, kiddo?" hollered Jeremy as he sprang down from the fence and headed into the main barn.

"Sure," mumbled Hilary, feeling slightly put out.

He seems really nice, but I'm most definitely not a kid. He looks my age. Could I really have been dreaming? No, I know I wasn't. Hilary's mind raced as she headed back to the east barn. *Better start my chores.*

She checked the cleaning list and began. Each stall had a number, making everything simple. She found the wheelbarrow and other tools in each barn and did her best. Since she had never done this before, she was uncertain about what to do. After a few stalls, however, she got the hang of it. By the time she finished, she was exhausted. Cleaning stalls really *was* hard work. She decided to go to the lounge, get a drink of cool water, and make some new friends. *Or so she thought.*

The lounge was located in the main barn. There were a couple of sofas, a refrigerator, and a bookshelf full of horse books. Students who had finished their riding lessons sat on the couches or stools by the small island that came out from the wall. They chatted noisily, discussing the day's lesson or their plans for tomorrow. Hilary felt left out when she got her drink and sat down. She didn't know any of the kids and nothing whatsoever about horses. Sitting in an empty arm chair, she listened to a conversation a group of girls was having.

"And can you believe how well Lady did the course?" said a small freckle-faced girl. "She flew over those jumps like a grasshopper."

"And she is so beautiful," joined in another.

"I wish Elise would let us ride Lady. It's not fair."

"I know. One day she said I could if I cleaned Lady's stall. So I did, and then she said it wasn't good enough, and wouldn't let me ride her," said a blonde-haired boy.

Hilary really didn't even know Elise, but by the sounds

of it, she wasn't a very nice person—not only to Hilary, but to other people as well. Finding nothing exciting in the lounge, she headed back to the east barn. Entering the stable, she saw Susan patting a muscular red-haired horse in the stall. A rubber line guarded the stall so the horse couldn't escape, but he could stick his head and neck out easily to nuzzle passersby for treats.

"Hey, Hilary, how's it going?" Susan asked, flashing a welcoming grin.

"Great, I completed all the stalls, and now I'm going to start the watering," Hilary said as she timidly patted the horse on the nose.

"Super, sounds like you're on top of everything. Oh, this is Lotto. You probably saw his stall identification," Susan said as she pointed to a check board on the stall door. "Lotto's a show jumper. He and I compete in events where we are timed while jumping a series of obstacles. He's very good at it, too," she explained, stroking his long face.

"That sounds like a lot of fun," Hilary said as she grabbed a water bucket to fill.

"Yes, it is. But it's challenging with a stallion like Lotto. Since he is a stallion, he can get very strong. He also likes to show off a little too much." She pointed to a picture on the check board of him running in a field. It gave Lotto's show name as Lucky Lottery. *How cute,* thought Hilary.

Before Susan left to teach, she showed Hilary exactly how to groom a horse, using Lotto for her demo. When she left, Hilary looked at the other four horses. Three of them were horses Susan was training. They were all a deep brown color, called seal bay on their check boards. In the last stall was Jeremy's horse, a steel gray named Splash. They were very attractive, too, but none of them matched the black horse's beauty.

Not too shabby, thought Hilary as she examined Lotto after his second grooming. His coat glimmered in the sunlight that reflected through the barn. Next Hilary groomed Splash, who was a bit on the pushy side. He frightened Hilary when he tried to search her for treats. Lastly, she groomed the three bays, Lilac, Star, and Carrousel. When she finally finished, she felt like an accomplished horsewoman. She was proud of herself for working so hard and surprised that she had actually enjoyed her first day at the farm. She couldn't wait for tomorrow.

That evening during dinner, Hilary was the center of attention. Her mom, dad, and brother asked questions about what she had done at the barn. Hilary bubbled with enthusiasm.

Later that night, she went upstairs and called Joy and Ali on the phone. She told them about her new job and asked how things were back home. She got all the latest gossip about Chris and told of her encounter with Jeremy. Finally, around eleven, Hilary hung up the phone and crawled into her bed. That night she slept straight through.

Chapter Five

*H*ilary was working in the south barn, sweeping the aisles and grooming the horses when Susan walked in and posted a notice on the bulletin board.

"Hey, Hilary. You've been working really hard."

"Yeah, I think I'm pretty much finished now," Hilary told her, putting the broom back where it belonged.

"I'd say so, too," Susan said approvingly, examining the barn. "So how were the horses today when you groomed them? Did Splash behave himself? He's a little greedy sometimes."

"Yes, they were all fine," Hilary answered, preoccupied. She hesitated then asked, "What's the deal with the black horse?"

"Oh, yes, I thought you might inquire about Satan," said Susan as she sat on a wooden trunk. "My friend gave me that horse thinking I could train him. Unfortunately, I'm not having much luck. He's a mustang from the adoption agency—and a stallion at that. The first day he got here we managed to get him in a field. He's torn up the grass, and he's a danger to my students. I just don't know what to do with him. He doesn't want anything to do with people." Susan was quiet for a minute then added, "At least he hasn't jumped the fence yet. I was kind of expecting he would."

Now Hilary was totally perplexed. *Had Satan jumped out of the paddock, and then jumped back in? He couldn't have possibly done that, not if he wanted to be free so badly.*

"Well, I better get home now. I'll see you tomorrow." Hilary said as she headed out of the barn. She passed Satan's paddock quietly and stared at the skinny, black horse. He wasn't eating his hay at all; he just stood staring at her, his eyes wary. Although he looked tall and powerful to Hilary, he was just fifteen hands. Susan had told her this was typical for mustangs.

That night Hilary had an eerie dream. She dreamt she was sitting in Satan's paddock singing to the troubled horse. He stood far away from her but watched her every move. Hilary read books to him, recited poems, and sang cheerful songs. The horse relaxed and began to walk toward her. She stood and walked to Satan's side. The horse nuzzled her arm, and she climbed on his back. A wide smile spread across her face and then vanished. Satan reared up on his powerful hind legs and sent Hilary crashing to the ground. He turned and veered toward her, showing no sign of slowing. The last things Hilary saw were his powerful hooves as they came crashing down on her.

Hilary sat up in her bed, drenched in sweat. She took a deep breath and looked out her window. Satan was pacing the fence quietly, doing no harm to anyone. She got up and went downstairs for a drink. Her father had already left for work so the kitchen was empty. She sat down quietly and sipped her cool water.

The next week went by smoothly. Hilary went to the barn each day and carried out her chores. She began to like working with the horses and even found herself at the barn on Sundays, her day off. Susan offered to give her a lesson in exchange for all her hard work, and Hilary gratefully accepted.

She rode the beginners' horse, Dolly, a spotted horse—an Appaloosa, Susan said—with a gentle temperament. She went willingly for Hilary with her head low and pace steady. They rode in the open sand arena, closest to the main barn. Susan was an amazing teacher, explaining everything clearly.

After the lesson was finished, she allowed Hilary to go out on a trail walk with a few other, more experienced riders. The woods made Hilary feel at peace with the world. Looking up into the canopy, she saw creatures flutter about; a sight that was new to her. Squirrels bounded from branch to branch, leaving the tree limbs rustling behind them, and the industrious sound of woodpeckers filled her ears. In Hilary's old surroundings, the only wildlife she ever saw was that which lay dead beside the busy roads of Delaware. The tranquility of the forest finally made Hilary feel at ease. The quiet gurgling of the brook, the whisper of trees in the summer breeze, and the other girls' murmurs of contentment added to the serenity.

She enjoyed her lesson so much, that for the first time in her life, Hilary wanted to ride horses. Later that evening, she phoned Susan to schedule a weekly lesson on Dolly. Susan agreed. Riding horses would be the first hobby for Hilary. The decision felt right, and she couldn't help but realize what a different girl she was becoming. It was as though the old Hilary was still in Delaware and had never made the trip to Lewisburg. A new girl was evolving.

"Good morning, Satan," chimed Hilary, as she walked to the barn one hot Wednesday morning. The horse just stared at her as he did every time she passed. To Hilary's knowledge, no one had been able to get near him, and the thought of returning Satan to Mary hung in the back of her mind. She figured Susan just wanted the horse to settle in a little more before she attempted to train him.

Wednesday was a slow day for lessons that week because most of the students were away on vacation. Elise, however, was at the barn every day, training for a major competition in the fall. Hilary tried to avoid her as she did her morning chores. But when Jeremy came into the barn, Elise was glued to his side.

"Hi there, Hilary," Elise said with a smirk. She and Jeremy halted in the aisle where Hilary was grooming Splash. "You look busy; your job must be hard. Don't get me wrong though, you fit it perfectly."

Jeremy acted as if he didn't hear the rude comment and asked, "So, how's Splash been?"

"He's doing well. I think he misses being ridden,

though," Hilary replied, as she lifted one of his feet to be cleaned. "He's getting a little rambunctious."

"Well, that won't be a problem anymore because Elise and I are going for a ride. Speaking of which"—Jeremy turned to Elise after glancing at his watch—"we better get going. I'll meet you in the field after we tack up our horses, okay?" Jeremy said.

"No, Jeri, Hilary can tack up Splash. Come with me, so I have company when I tack Lady. Now come on," she said, tugging on Jeremy's arm.

He asked Hilary, "Do you mind?"

Hilary lied and said she didn't. The truth she wasn't sure she remembered how. Susan had shown her once for her lesson last week, but that was it. She tried her best though and finished putting Splash's bridle on, just as Jeremy came back.

"Thanks, Hilary," he said as he checked the tightness of the girth. He swung his leg over the saddle, and he and Elise cantered across the gravel and into the lush, green field. *You're welcome,* thought Hilary as she got Carrousel out of his stall and began his grooming.

By the time four o' clock rolled around, Hilary was hot and sweaty. Her white tee-shirt clung to her dampened skin leaving her conscious of how see-through the shirt appeared. Despite that, she tacked up Dolly for her lesson. Susan said they'd work on Hilary's position, explaining that the rider comes first. "You can't expect the horse to be good if you aren't good yourself."

Susan set up some cones and had Hilary bend back and forth between them. It was a fun lesson, and once again, Hilary was allowed to join in on the trail hack with some other students. They took the Water Brooke trail, and Hilary found it even more exhilarating to ride through a stream than it had been to ride past one. To a city girl from Delaware, this was fascinating. Everything was new, but unlike her first few days in Lewisburg, Tennessee, this was new in a good way. She made a few friends with some of the other riders, even if they were a few years younger than she was.

After Hilary returned to the stables and took care of Dolly, she headed across the barnyard to see Satan. As usual, the horse paced along the fence. Hilary called his name and was surprised to see him look over at her. That's a start, she thought.

During dinner that night, Hilary discussed what she did in her lesson that day.

"It was really fun, but you know what? I think I should get some real riding clothes, instead of jeans and sneakers. Everyone else has riding attire, and I look weird without any."

"I think that's a fabulous idea, Hilary," said Karen. Hilary knew her mom was happy that she had finally found a sport she liked. "How about we go tomorrow when you finish your jobs at the barn. Does that sound good?"

"Great," exclaimed Hilary.

Chapter Six

Hilary knew exactly what to look for in the store after talking to some of the kids at the farm. She asked them what types of boots and riding pants to get. She made a list so she wouldn't forget what they were.

Things to get at the tack shop:
1. *Brown paddock boots*
2. *Tan riding breeches (jodhpurs)*
3. *Brown riding gloves – to match my boots*
4. *Riding socks – with horses on them*
5. *If mom will let me – a sweat absorbent T-shirt*

When she became a more talented rider she'd ask her mom to buy her tall boots and white breeches like Elise had. Thinking of Elise made Hilary cringe with irritation. She always had to be the center of attention, and all the younger students looked up to her like she was a goddess. Hilary hoped they would admire her when she became a skilled equestrian.

"We're here, Hil," said Karen, grabbing her purse and getting out of the car. Hilary walked eagerly into the store. It smelled of leather and newly polished tack. She began searching for the items on her list. Hilary found a nice pair of boots, breeches, and gloves, and tried them on at least twice.

Around dusk, Hilary decided to visit Satan. She didn't know why she wanted to, but something kept telling her he needed a friend.

Accompanying Hilary was a book on beginner riding that Susan had suggested. She sat under the large oak tree next to Satan's paddock. As soon as she began reading aloud, Satan turned and walked away to the far end of the paddock. Hilary didn't let it bother her, though, and continued as if he were right beside her.

She didn't know how long she read to him, but when she finally set the book down it was nearly dark. "Wow, time flies when you're having fun, huh, boy?" she said, standing up and brushing grass clippings off her jeans. "Well, goodnight, Satan. I'll see you in the morning."

Hilary decided to make reading to Satan a must for every day. *I'll tame this horse if it's the last thing I do.*

Hilary was tidying up her desk when the phone in her room rang. It was Susan, and she wanted to speak with Karen. "Is your mom there?" she asked.

"Yes, she's here," Hilary said as she hurtled down the stairs and handed her mother the phone. Hilary went back up to her room and waited for Karen to explain why Susan had called. Finally, after what seemed like hours, her mom tapped quietly on her door.

"I've got some news for you, young lady," Karen said, entering and sitting down on Hilary's bed. "The girl who's been riding Dolly everyday just left for summer camp in the Poconos. Susan wondered if you want to lease Dolly so you can ride her whenever you want. Would you like that?"

Hilary lost her breath but recovered quickly and accepted Susan's offer. All she had to do was be responsible for Dolly's grooming and stall, and she could ride all she wanted.

That night Hilary had another haunting dream. It was just like the one she had before, except this time, it went further. She had been reading to Satan, and just like before, the horse walked over to her. Hilary got up and began stroking him on his neck. Next, she climbed onto his back and smiled, reaching out to pat Satan once more. Just as she did so, the black horse took off through the night, and easily soared over the wooden fence. Satan was moving so fast that Hilary couldn't even see. The colors were all blurred, and tears blinded her eyes as they galloped and galloped. After what seemed like endless running, Satan slowed to a trot and then a walk. Hilary quickly dismounted and ran from the black horse. He chased her. She couldn't get out of his way in time, and just as in the first dream, his hooves darkened her vision.

Chapter Seven

"Then you must square your shoulders to the horse, hunch them over and wait for the horse to come to you," Hilary read, glancing up to look at Satan. "Would you like to do a join-up, boy?" she asked, knowing the horse would not respond. Observing the expression on his face, she knew he didn't want anything to do with her. She moved slightly closer to the fence and leaned against it, facing him. He stood at the far end of the paddock glaring at her. She wondered whether he would ever accept her presence. *One day,* she thought, staring at Satan. *One day.*

Later, Hilary closed the book on riding basics and headed for her house. As she passed through the thicket of trees near her home she heard a horse nicker softly. Hilary swore her heart skipped ten beats. She slowly turned around and, unable to believe what she saw, stepped closer to Satan's paddock.

Satan stood a little way from the fence, staring at Hilary, *Oh my gosh! He wants me to stay.* Hilary had dreamt of this day for some time, but for some reason she didn't know what to do. Should she go over to him and try to pet him, or should she continue for home? Without any more hesitation, the decision was made. She would go home, so he would think about her and wish she were still there. That way, when she visited him on the way to the stables the next morning, he would be happy to have her company. She would begin taking him carrots and sugar cubes and maybe even apples. He would like that.

"Hey there, Satan," Hilary greeted, as she leaned over the fence the next morning. She'd had another dream that night, but for the first time it hadn't ended badly. Hilary had simply read to the horse the whole time and stroked him once or twice. Then it was over. That gave her more confidence for her meeting with him today.

Satan glanced in her direction and held her stare for a couple of minutes before looking away. *Well, that's kind of an improvement,* she thought as she sat under the big oak and opened her book. "And that's definitely an improvement!" she said quietly, watching Satan take a step toward her end of the paddock. Not wanting to stop him from coming, she continued reading as though the most remarkable thing hadn't just occurred. Again he stepped toward her. She couldn't resist it any longer. She stood up and called to him. *That makes three,* she thought, counting the number of steps he took in her direction. Knowing she shouldn't push her luck, she slid an apple under the paddock fence for him.

"See ya, handsome, I better get to work."

Hilary strode to the barn, anxious to begin her chores. She figured she would take Dolly out on the trails around twelve. It was going to be hot though, so she decided to take the Woodland trail, which led to the very depth of the forest. It was cool there, and she had never followed it all the way, but today she would.

"Good morning," called a few kids in friendly greeting as they passed on their way to lessons. Hilary smiled and proceeded to the south barn's notice board. Everyday she checked it and wrote down the stall numbers that needed cleaning. Susan was right; she did have some lazy boarders. Today, however, only five additional stalls would be added to her list. *Yes!*

As she headed over to the east barn, she saw someone hanging around Satan's paddock. Hilary could make out the figure right away. It was Jeremy, and he seemed to be talking to Satan. *But why?* Veering off her own trail, she headed over to see what he was up to.

"Hey," Jeremy said. "Nice morning, isn't it?"

"Yeah, it's already hot, though."

"Yup," he replied, turning back to look at Satan.

Noticing Jeremy wasn't too interested in starting a conversation, Hilary turned to walk away. But then she remembered what she'd really come here to ask. Tossing her hair from her shoulder, she turned around and looked Jeremy square in the eye.

"By the way, what are you doing with Satan?" she asked, pulling herself up on the fence next to him.

"I'm trying to make him my friend, you know, tame him. He'll come around some day."

"Yeah, but your mom said that she was gonna send

him back to Mary if he didn't come around soon," Hilary said, brushing a strand of loose hair from her eyes.

"Well, it's all up to me, really. She just told me that."

"What do you mean?"

"I mean it's my decision."

"Your decision to keep him? How come it's not your mom's?"

"Because he's my horse! My mom gave him to me to train. She said he'd been ridden a few times before but needed some work. Then, if I get him going, I can ride him in the Junior Jumper's Final this fall. That's what everyone's training for now." Hilary was dumbfounded. *Satan belongs to Jeremy?*

"Why don't you just ride Splash?" Hilary asked.

"He can't jump for his life. I've had him for seven years, and he's already sixteen. Plus he's a quarter horse, not an athletic sport horse," Jeremy finished, pointing to Satan in the far corner of the paddock. "And he…"

"He ate it!" Hilary said aloud, noticing that the apple she'd placed in the pen that morning was gone.

"What are you talking about?" Jeremy asked, staring at Hilary.

"Oh, just…nothing."

"Okay, so anyway," he continued, "Satan is just the horse I need to compete in the Jumper's Final. The only problem is time. I won't have enough time to work with him because the finals are at the end of August," he said, a frown on his face.

"Oh my gosh," Hilary said, "that stinks."

Jeremy nodded and turned to look at Satan once more. The horse was at the far end of the paddock near the spot Hilary had sat earlier that day. He was gazing in the opposite direction, but Hilary sensed he was listening to their every word. "Well, I better get to work," she said. Jeremy nodded and continued observing his horse.

As she was passing one of the lesson arenas, Hilary paused to watch the students ride a course of jumps.

"Very nice, Nicole, just remember to keep your eyes up and your heels down," instructed Elise, clearly frustrated with the younger students. "Now it's your turn, Stacy," she said. Noticing Hilary, she stepped over to where she was watching the lesson.

"Hi there, teaching lessons is great, isn't it? Oh wait, you've never had the pleasure of doing so," she smirked, flashing her straight, white teeth. "Well, I am a fabulous teacher, so I could teach you how to teach."

"Maybe some other time. I'd better get back to work," Hilary responded, beginning to walk away.

"Suit yourself, Hilary, but you're being rather foolish. It's not like you have much to do," Elise taunted. "I think you just don't want to be out in the heat."

Hilary started to defend herself, but Elise cut her off. "So in that case..." she began, smiling, "why don't you come swimming with me at the creek. You know, a little one on one time. It'll make up for us getting off to such a bad start."

Hilary doubted anything could ever make up for their "bad start" together, but, as she was in no position to pass up friends, she accepted Elise's invitation.

"Great. I'll see you around one-thirty by the creek on the Woodland trail," and with that Elise swung her long, golden hair over her shoulder and returned to her lesson. "What a great round that was, Nicole. You looked very balanced." The little girl rolled her eyes, obviously realizing Elise hadn't caught a glimpse of it. Hilary stifled a giggle.

Back in the stable, she tackled her chores. It was hot now, so Hilary looked forward to swimming. *Darn*, she thought, wiping her salty face, *I need my bathing suit.* Hilary jogged back past the main barn toward her house. She slowed to a walk when she passed Satan, who was pacing the fence near the large oak tree. Seeing the moving figure startled him, and he cantered to the center of the corral. Hilary continued to her house and ran upstairs to her room. She grabbed her bathing suit and pulled her hair down from a soggy bun. After quickly brushing it, she slapped sunscreen on her face and tugged her bathing suit on under her riding clothes. She had to admit she was looking forward to making up with Elise. *Maybe she isn't so bad after all.*

"See ya," Hilary called to the vacant house as she rushed out the door.

Chapter Eight

*D*olly was a placid horse. She walked calmly along the path doing everything Hilary asked. She never spooked or tried to snatch a bite of grass, and she obeyed all the commands Hilary gave her. During the previous lesson, Susan had allowed her to trot. Everyday that followed, Hilary had gotten better at the bumpy, two-beat motion. Now she barely even bounced. Overall, she had become much more accustomed to the feel of a horse beneath her, especially if that horse was Dolly.

Hilary heard voices up ahead. *So we're finally here,* she thought as she rounded the bend. She saw Lady and Splash tied to a large tree branch. *Great, so Jeremy is here, too,* she thought, uncertain if it was a good thing or a bad thing. She dismounted, wound Dolly's reins around a limb near the other horses, and tried to figure out where Elise and Jeremy had gone. She heard a soft voice mutter something behind a boulder. At a snail's pace, she climbed up the rock and, careful to stay hidden, peeked through the brush. She saw Elise and Jeremy sitting in a large pool of water splashing each other playfully.

"Don't be silly, Jer, you know I can't beat you."

"You never know, you look like a fast swimmer," he replied, a smile spreading across his handsome face.

"You're just trying to butter me up so I will race you. And you know I don't like to race whether it be a horse race or a foot race," Elise said, pulling her hair back from her face and twisting it around her fingers. Jeremy laughed at her. Hilary was just about to announce her arrival when she glanced over at the horses, who were getting restless. When she looked back at Jeremy and Elise, she changed her mind. *No way will I join them now.* Their lips were touching lightly, and Elise's hand was wrapped around Jeremy's neck. They were kissing!

Hilary was angry, feeling sure that Elise had invited her up here just to make her jealous. And if the truth be told, she had succeeded. Hilary hurled herself down from the rocks and sprinted over to Dolly. She untied the mare, climbed into the saddle, and pushed Dolly into a fast trot. As the anger subsided, Hilary realized she was cantering.

"We're cantering, Dolly," she exclaimed, trying to move with the motion of her horse. It was an amazing feeling. The light breeze caressed her tired face, and the quiet thump, thump, thump, of Dolly's hooves helped Hilary to stay in rhythm with the horse. She held herself in jumping position as Susan had taught her to help strengthen her leg muscles. When she returned home, Karen took her to buy her own set of tack at the Lewisburg Saddlery. She chose a flashy bridle and saddle, each rich chocolate in color, and a matching girth.

"Despite my little run-in with Jeremy and Elise, it wasn't a half-bad day. Dolly was great and I got to canter," Hilary explained to Satan that evening as she sat under the oak.

He stood, as usual, at the far end of the paddock, but unlike every other day, he watched her and even looked curious at Hilary's gabbling. "But I'm sure Elise only invited me so I would see the two of them together. On second thought, how about I don't talk about that? Here you go, boy." Hilary reached into a duffel bag and rolled an apple into the paddock, careful not to spook the horse. It stopped about two feet from him. He snorted and backed away.

Hilary had finished the book on basic riding and borrowed another one, *The Rider's Seat,* from the lounge. She began to read but kept a close eye on Satan to see if he'd eat the apple. After five minutes or so, he stepped tentatively forward and took the apple in his mouth. Hilary stopped reading aloud and watched as he ate it. Foam from the juicy fruit frothed around his muzzle, and she laughed out loud.

"Silly boy, Satan," she said as she picked up the book and continued reading. Satan seemed to listen the whole time and even came to stand in the center of the paddock. When she finished, she told him all about the happenings in her life until it seemed that she had nothing further to tell her new friend.

"It's getting dark, boy. I have to go home, okay?" she said, picking up her books and taking one last look at the stallion. She smiled to herself and started toward the house. Her mother's car pulled in the driveway.

"Hi, Mom," she called out.

"Hello, Hil. You can congratulate your brother; he just won his baseball game." Karen smiled, opening the door to the house and heading in. "We're going out for dinner tonight so wash up." Sam scampered in behind her, leaving Hilary alone. She turned back and looked at Satan. He had his neck pressed against the fence closest to her house as though he wanted to follow her. Hilary's heart leapt. *He wants to be with me! I have to stay with him.*

She dashed up the porch and flung open the front door. Immediately she skidded to a halt. Slowly, she sauntered down the hall and into the kitchen.

"Mom, I don't feel well. I'm tired, and I think I'm dehydrated," she fibbed, trying her hardest to look ill.

"You don't look well, Hilary. You're pale. Maybe you should stay home," Karen said, putting her hand to her daughter's forehead, "although you're not feverish."

Hilary frowned, "Oh, but I want to go."

"No, dear, I think you should stay. I'll bring back some soup for you. Now go on up to bed and get some rest. And drink plenty of water."

Hilary watched from her bedroom window as Karen and Sam settled into the Nissan and drove out of sight. She shifted her gaze from the driveway to Satan's corral. Pacing up and down the fence line nearest the Thompsons' house, the horse looked lonesome. Hilary rushed down the stairs and grabbed some apples from the kitchen. She made her way to the paddock.

"I'm here, boy," she cooed, rolling an apple under the fence. For the first time Satan didn't snort, and he didn't back away, nor did he hesitate to consume the apple. After he was finished, he stepped toward Hilary, probably looking for more food. She was leaning against the rail fence, and Satan nervously sniffed her hair and then her clothes. He blew warm air out of his nostrils. Hilary talked to him quietly before making her first attempt to pet him. She slowly pulled her hand out from under his nose and reached out to caress his face. He backed away nervously, but when Hilary didn't attempt to get any closer to him, he stepped nearer once again, and pressed his nose into the palm of her hand. This time he let her stroke his face and then his neck. She couldn't believe her luck! After a few more minutes of petting him, she headed to the house. *I want to end on a good note.*

Chapter Nine

*H*ilary visited Satan each morning, treating him to an apple and a few pats. In the evening, careful to let no one see, she read aloud from a book on riding, talked of her day, and stroked him all over. Later in the week she entered his paddock. He didn't try to hurt her at all and didn't avoid her either. He followed Hilary around like a little puppy in need of attention.

So far, she had been lucky. Karen normally ran errands in the afternoon and picked Sam up from his sports, so she wasn't aware of Hilary's taming sessions. Nor was Susan or anybody at the stables, for Satan's paddock was nestled away from the commotion of the farm.

However, many of the students hung around Satan's paddock, admiring his beauty and wishing they could ride him. They had made it part of their daily routine to go say, "Hi," to him each morning. It was strange to Hilary that he still stayed as far away from them as possible. Apparently he would only let Hilary near him. That caused her to bubble with joy. Maybe she was being selfish, wanting him only for herself, but after all, it was she who had worked to earn his trust.

In her lesson, Susan viewed Hilary's progress in posting and rewarded it by letting her canter. It wasn't bad for what Susan thought was Hilary's first time. Hilary had been unable to resist practicing Dolly's canter in the fields.

On Saturday, the barn was packed with people, for riding camps had started. Elise was aiding Susan in teaching some of the lessons, so she rarely had time to give Hilary trouble, although she had antagonized her for a few minutes on Thursday.

"I saw you spying on Jeri and me the other day," she'd said as she passed Hilary in the barn, "at the creek, you know. You just better keep your distance. I'm warning you. I know you like Jeremy; all the girls here do—even at school. He and I are the most popular couple in our grade."

Hilary sat in the field with Satan thinking back on all her troubles with Elise. *Why does she have to be such a pain? Does she think I'm a threat or something?*

Hilary pondered this for some time before she went about stroking Satan. She slid her hands gently over his delicate face, legs, and back, getting him accustomed to her every touch. After this process, she looked around to make sure no one was watching. Out of her duffel bag, she took a soft, leather halter that belonged to Dolly.

"This should fit you," she said, entering the small paddock. She rubbed the halter all over Satan's body until he didn't quiver at its touch. Then she allowed him to sniff it and fed him a carrot as she held the halter under his muzzle. "Good boy," she murmured as she slipped the halter snuggly behind his ears. Satan didn't seem to notice.

Hilary pulled a lead rope from the bag and clipped it to the bottom of the halter. She walked forward in an effort to teach Satan to follow. She didn't even have to tug on the line to get the trusting horse to follow her—he just did. But Hilary realized that Satan would follow her whether she had a lead rope or not. So she tried tugging on it and, as though she had fired a shot, Satan threw his head in the air. "Easy, boy, settle down now," she soothed, stroking his head. She resumed by applying the tiniest bit of pressure on his halter, and before long, he followed her calmly once again.

After a few more minutes of training, a light flickered on in the main barn. A black figure, silhouetted in the bright light, ran toward her. Not wanting whoever it was to see what she was doing, she ripped off Satan's halter and shoved her things into the bag. She took off for the house.

As she was running, she realized how imprudent it was to go straight to her own home. Satan watched her leave and whinnied as she closed the front door behind her. Inside, she found her mom, dad, and Sam eating dinner at the table. Her sudden entrance alarmed them all, and Karen leapt from her seat and looked her straight in the eye. *Oh boy.*

"Where have you been, Hilary Lee Thompson?" Karen demanded. Hilary cringed at the sound of her middle name. Her mom only said that when she was *really* angry. "Your father and I have been worried sick!"

"I know, Mom, I'm really sorry but I wanted to…chat with Susan for a while and tell her how things are going with Dolly," Hilary lied, doing her best to look sincere. She realized she'd been doing a lot of fibbing lately, but rationalized that it was for a good cause and therefore okay, though it didn't feel quite right.

"Well, all right, but you'll have to eat your food cold because we've been waiting forever." Karen sat down and began eating her corn-on-the-cob. Hilary nodded and moved her plate to the microwave oven.

That night she was awakened by a sudden thud from outside. *What on earth?* she thought. Jumping up, she peered at the ground below her windowsill.

"Satan!" Hilary shrieked.

Chapter Ten

Someone stood, arms waving, in the center of Satan's corral. Hilary stampeded down the stairs, her shoulder-length hair streaking behind her. She had to find out why this person was antagonizing the stallion and put a stop to it.

She wore only a cream-colored slip which she wore on nights when her pajamas no longer suited the weather. Her thin legs covered the dewy ground with hasty strides as the tears that welled in her eyes became hot and painful. *Who was doing this to Satan? And why?*

Hilary reflected on the previous evening when she had seen a dark figure coming toward Satan and her. Then another recollection seeped into her mind; the night she saw Satan jump the fence. *Was someone trying to hurt him? And will he jump the fence again?* Hilary brushed these thoughts aside as she reached the fence and launched herself over the top post.

"What are you doing?" she hollered, brushing her wavy hair out of her face. Her bare toes found traction on the dirt-covered paddock, and she surged toward the person standing in the middle. She tried to decelerate, but she only skidded over some dry grass and slammed into the figure.

"What the—!" the person grunted and hit the ground with a thump. Hilary, unable to keep her balance, fell on top of him.

"Hilary?" he asked, sounding horrified. She looked down at Jeremy and pushed herself away from him in disgust.

"What are you doing to Satan?" she gasped, as Jeremy sat up and stared her in the eye.

"He's my horse, Hilary. Why don't you tell me why you crashed into me? You trying to save my horse from his owner?" he finished, a smile creeping over his face like the Cheshire Cat.

"I'm sorry; I didn't know it was you," Hilary blurted, looking at Satan in the far end of the paddock. He was lathered in sweat and breathing heavily through his flaring nostrils. "But what are you doing to him?"

"A join-up. Ever heard of one?"

"Of course I've heard of one. What do you think I am, an idiot?" she replied swiftly, boiling with anger.

"Whoa, whoa now. Take a chill pill. It was only a question, kid."

"Would you stop calling me a kid? I'm the same age as you, I'm sure." Hilary was really mad now.

"Yeah, I bet you are. Now cool it; you're going to wake up the whole state of Tennessee," Jeremy breathed. "So, let me get this straight, you thought I was trying to hurt Satan?"

"Yes, actually, I did. Why, is there something wrong with me?"

"No, no," Jeremy said quickly, "but I assure you, I was only trying to befriend him through a join-up." He laughed and pointed to the horse huddled in the corner. "As you can see, it's not going too great."

"Yes, I can see that. If I were you, I would stop trying to do this join-up thing with Satan. You're scaring him even more," Hilary said as she started toward the horse.

But then she realized she couldn't let Jeremy know she'd been trying to tame his horse. He would probably be furious, especially if he knew how much Satan already trusted her. She turned around and looked Jeremy straight in the eyes.

"Leave him alone," she said, and with great effort, she went back to her home.

Hilary groomed Dolly at the barn early the next morning. It was another hot day, and she wanted to get her ride in before the real heat set in. It was Monday, and she had devised a weekly schedule the night before for what she should do in her rides each week. Today, according to her schedule, she planned to do trotting exercises in the main grass ring.

Hilary warmed up the appaloosa by walking her around a few times. Then she picked up a rising trot, doing her best to maintain her balance. She practiced circles, figure eights and even serpentines, following Susan's instructions.

After about an hour, Hilary led Dolly back to the barn. She hosed the mare off and returned her to her stall. She went to the notice board in the front of the barn to see which stalls needed cleaning. Before she had a chance to scan through the list, Hilary saw brochures pinned to the board and picked one off.

Millbrooke Stables' Summer Horse Show
Saturday July, 16th: $15 per class

Lead Line:	Equitation:
Walk, walk-trot, walk-trot poles	Beginner walk - trot, Amateur walk-trot, w-t-c, w-t-c over 2' fences
Pleasure:	
Walk-trot, walk-trot-canter, w-t-rein back, young horse hack	Hunter:
	Green horse, 18", 2', 2'3, 2'6, 3', 3'6

A smile spread across Hilary's face. But the sixteenth was right around the corner. *Will I have enough time to prepare? What classes should I enter? I'll have to ask Susan,* she thought, already anticipating the event.

Realizing how parched she was, Hilary headed for the lounge to get a glass of ice water. There, she spotted Jeremy and Elise on the sofas talking to Susan.

"He was great last night, too, Mom, he even let me pet him a couple of times," Jeremy said as he sipped ice tea. Hilary knew he was referring to Satan, and he was lying.

"Good, I'm so happy. I guess we won't be giving him back to Mary after all then, will we? She called a couple nights ago and said, if all is well, you can keep him. You know she cares about you a lot, Jer. She's like some fairy godmother, giving you that horse," finished Susan, patting Jeremy's knee and standing up. "I'm going to ride Lotto. I'll see you later."

Hilary was surprised that none of the kids in the lounge jumped up to follow Susan. *Don't they want to watch her ride? I sure do.* Hilary darted after Susan.

"Susan, may I watch you ride?" Hilary called across the aisle.

"Well, Hil, I don't normally let the students watch me ride—it's a bit distracting. I try to ride in the indoor, where all is calm and cool," Susan said, smiling.

"Okay, that's fine," Hilary responded, feeling a little put out.

"But you know, I am jumping today, and it would be a good learning experience for you. So why don't you come along? Just don't tell the other students," she laughed.

Hilary nodded, surprised by Susan's exception to the rule. As Susan tacked Lotto, Hilary began mucking out his stall and loading it with fresh straw. When the horses stayed in all day, they made their stalls quite dirty, but Hilary found it relaxing to clean as she could easily let her mind wander. When Susan was ready, the trio walked into the indoor arena located in the center of the property. Hilary gasped as she stepped into the large ring. There were jumps standing at least five feet high throughout the whole arena. She sat in the bleachers, sipping from a water bottle she'd brought along.

"We have horse shows in here during the winter. It works out wonderfully. You should set one of the jumping classes as a goal for you and Dolly," Susan said as she pulled herself gracefully into the saddle. "Speaking of which, did you see the pamphlet for the summer show I set out in the main barn?"

Hilary nodded. "I've been meaning to ask you what classes I should enter," she said. "It looks like fun."

"It is—for the riders at least! It's a lot of work on my part, quite honestly," Susan said, as she walked Lotto out to the track. "But the students always have a great time. It's one of the highlights of the summer." Looking back at Hilary, she added, "I'd say you and Dolly should shoot for the walk-trot-canter class."

Hilary nodded but was soon completely mesmerized by Susan's riding ability. Everything looked so simple when she walked, trotted, and cantered Lotto around the ring. Susan was so relaxed in the saddle that Hilary could tell she was more than just a good rider; she was a star. Lotto jumped every fence with room to spare. He was powerful in all his moves, and Susan was a skilled rider. Hilary wanted to be just like her. *When I finish taming Satan, we will jump, too,* Hilary thought.

Thinking about Satan made her face light up. But the

brightness soon dimmed as she remembered what Jeremy had told his mom earlier that day. *Did Susan actually believe Jeremy's made-up story? He was totally faking it.* Hilary thought it over for a while then decided she'd figured it out. Jeremy must want Satan so badly, he made up that story to keep his mom from returning the horse. Like Hilary, he made up lies in order to keep Satan safe. She hoped it wouldn't come back to bite them. Jeremy wanted Satan's trust. So did she. Just that morning on her way to the barn, she read the little stallion a short chapter out of a book. Then she gave him carrots and a few pats. She would try to spend more time with him in the evening when no one was around.

When Hilary finally finished her barn chores, it was late afternoon. She decided to get some items from the stables to present to Satan. She borrowed a small pony saddle, which was lighter than her own. She was surprised and relieved when the little girl didn't ask why she wanted her saddle. She grabbed an old pad and some apples. Now she was ready to begin Satan's evening training session.

When Hilary reached his paddock, she remained on the outside of the fence as she read *Breaking the Young Horse,* which she'd borrowed from Susan's collection. The dark horse stood next to the fence near her. After fifteen minutes of reading, she stood up and handed him an apple. He took it gingerly and rubbed her hand for more. She laughed as she climbed the fence into the paddock.

Hilary began by massaging his legs and body to remind him of her touch. She knew she couldn't start real training until dark for fear of people from the barn watching. So while she waited for time to pass, she went back to her book. When it was dark enough that she could begin working with Satan, Hilary led him around the small corral with a halter and a lead rope. Next, she rubbed his back until she felt he wouldn't mind the pad. As she placed it on his back he turned around and eyed her suspiciously. She just laughed and continued working.

Within twenty minutes, Hilary had the tiny saddle resting on Satan's back. He didn't seem to mind one bit. Hilary thought he was enjoying the attention. She soon came to the conclusion that someone must have put a saddle on him before, but she also concluded that it must not have ended well. Why else would a horse be so afraid of people? Thinking back to Hilary's first day in Tennessee and her first time seeing Satan, she recalled the old lady, Mary, talking about a man named Robert. Hilary was sure Mary told Susan that he'd ridden the mustang.

Nevertheless, Hilary wanted to take things slowly. Her understanding of horses was growing, and she knew she mustn't rush her training with Satan. And so, after leading him around the paddock a few times, she decided to end the session.

Chapter Eleven

"Why don't we begin with a nice rising trot around the ring? Make sure you are soft with your hands, and your heels remain down and quiet," Susan called as Hilary trotted Dolly around the outdoor arena.

Hilary felt like a very classy rider. That morning her mom had signed and delivered Hilary's entry for the show, and it seemed like all the lessons from Susan were really starting to pay off. Hilary cantered, practicing circles and straight lines. Susan told her she had her basic balance down pat, but she still needed to work on swinging her hips in the motion of Dolly's movement. Susan also told her to borrow a book entitled, *Cantering for Beginners*, from her collection.

Hilary saddled Satan with her own new saddle, that evening, because she felt he had graduated to a more substantial one. She began as she normally did, reading a chapter from a book, and then rubbing the horse's body and legs. Next she placed the pad on his back and then the saddle. Finally she fastened the girth and walked Satan around the paddock.

He walked quietly behind her, his head held low. He didn't do one thing wrong, so, after five minutes, Hilary untacked him. She planned to head to her house and have some dinner, but Satan had other ideas. As she climbed the fence, he grabbed her shirt with his teeth and gave it a tug.

"Satan!" squealed Hilary, hopping down from the fence and smiling. "You want me to stay don't you?" Satan bobbed his head playfully, as though he were nodding a reply. She scratched him on the head, which he enjoyed for a minute before pulling away and prancing to the other end of the paddock. He looked back at her and tossed his head once more. *He wants me to play with him!* Hilary laughed and skipped after the mischievous mustang.

They must have played for at least an hour. It was the funniest game you could play with a horse. When Hilary would catch up with Satan, he would throw his head into the air and canter after her. At first she was startled by his playfulness, but she soon learned he didn't mean to hurt her. She was sorry when it was time to say goodnight.

The day of the farm show quickly arrived. Hilary went to the stables early that morning, retrieved Dolly from her pasture, and spent a long time grooming her to make sure she sparkled with cleanliness.

The rest of the students were hard at work, too. Everyone was animated as they bustled around readying their mounts for the competition. Bright smiles shone on their faces, even though they confessed to butterflies fluttering in their stomachs. Susan ran the registration desk where all the riders received their numbers and riding times.

Hilary began to feel butterflies, too, as her first class loomed closer. She warmed Dolly up just as she would for a regular lesson, but when the loud speaker crackled, she brought Dolly to a halt.

"Class number five is to ride into the arena at this time. I repeat: Class number five to the ring at this time." Hilary's heart leapt. Her first class was the walk-trot equitation. She was feeling pretty confident until she reached the ring. There were at least fifteen horses in the class. *I'll be lucky if the judges even notice me,* thought Hilary as she took her place on the rail. As she scanned her competitors, she realized that she was a few years older than the rest. That thought brought back the butterflies. *What if they all beat me? I'll be so embarrassed.*

Before her nerves could overcome her, the announcer called out, "Walk please, all walk." Hilary tried her best to keep a bright smile on her face, as Karen had advised her to do, and worked her hardest to look in good form. She saw her mom smiling from the side of the ring and quickly looked away. *I have to concentrate.*

"Trot, please, all trot." Hilary picked up a posting trot and sunk her heels as deep as possible. After a few minutes the announcer told the group to reverse directions at the trot. Then they were asked to come back to a walk and face the judge. *Oh great, here come the ribbons.* Hilary thought back on her performance. It wasn't the best she'd ever done, but it surely wasn't the worst.

"Honorable mentions go to numbers forty-two, thirty-nine, ninety-five and twenty-two." That was Hilary's number. Twenty-two. She hadn't even received a ribbon. Gloomily, she walked Dolly out of the ring and back to the warm-up area. After a few minutes Karen came bounding up to her and said, "What a terrific job you did, honey. That was outstanding." Karen was clearly trying to make her feel better.

"Thanks, Mom." Hilary smiled, amused by how hard her mom was trying. "I'll see you in a few minutes, okay? My next class is number seven, walk-trot-canter."

Hilary rode Dolly into the ring, determined to do better. She put on a big smile and sat up nice and tall. Her trot work was all right, but her canter was better. She swung easily with Dolly's movement and tried her best not to bounce. When the class was completed, she was certain she placed in the top three.

"Tenth place goes to number twenty-two, Hilary Thompson, riding That Darn Dolly." Hilary couldn't believe it. She thought she had done so well in that class, yet she placed last. *At least I didn't get an honorable mention,* she thought, trying to smile. Most people would be discouraged if they basically lost both classes, but Hilary was determined. She wanted to make Susan proud to be her instructor, and, one day, she would show all those people how good she really was.

But right now, Hilary just wanted to see Satan. She didn't want to hang around the barn any longer, so after she completed her chores, she left for his corral. She saw him pacing the fence below her window and was immediately overcome with joy. Just seeing his familiar black figure was enough to heal her deepest wounds. However, the horse show must have really upset him, for he was covered in a light sweat.

"Easy now, Satan. I'm here, boy." Hilary soothed, climbing the paddock fence and stroking the nervous horse. She began by massaging his muscles in an effort to ease the tension. Then she patted his neck and left for the house. She would have to wait until evening when the stables weren't so overrun.

After the sweltering sun had set, Hilary made her way to Satan once more. She placed the halter over his ears and led him around the paddock. Once he was completely settled, she put the saddle pad and then the saddle over his back. Next she fastened the girth and made it as tight as it would allow. Satan didn't like this much, she could tell, but he stood perfectly still. She then allowed him to follow her at his own free will. They walked around for ten minutes before she untacked him, having decided they should end their session. "Good night, boy. I'll see you later."

In bed, Hilary's thoughts drifted back to her old life, so far away. It was like she was a whole new person now that she had horses in her life. It gave her something to strive for. When she had checked the messages from Ali and Joy earlier that night, she felt no real urge to call them back. Of course she would; it was just that things were working out so well for her at her new home. She was spending much more time outdoors and away from the computer. Back in Delaware, she had turned on her computer as soon as she got home from school. She spent the rest of her day sending Instant Messages to all her friends. Thinking back on those days, Hilary realized how much she had grown up in just the past few weeks.

But her old memories soon escaped her, and she was left with images of Satan. Unable to think of anything else, she decided she would return to him later that night when no one could observe the session. She would teach him to carry a rider.

Chapter Twelve

At midnight Hilary's alarm broke the peaceful stillness. She silenced it quickly, not wanting to wake her family, and scrambled out of bed. She put on her old jeans and boots and tied her hair back into a messy ponytail. She sped down the winding stairs, being careful not to hit the squeaky parts. Once she was safely outdoors, she looked for Satan in the small enclosure. He stood near the large oak tree as though he knew she would come. When he saw her, he gave a nicker of welcome and tossed his head into the air. Hilary made her way to the fence and slowly slipped between the boards and inside.

She began this session as she had all the others. Once Satan was tacked up, except for the bridle, she led him to the fence. First, Hilary leaned some of her weight onto the saddle, as she had seen demonstrated in a book. She gradually increased the load until her whole body was draped across the horse's back. Satan didn't seem to mind, yet he was curious about what she was doing.

"Easy now, babe." Hilary smiled, as he turned his head around to nibble her back. She could hardly believe Satan was allowing her to ride him—well, almost. It was only a matter of time before she could actually spread her legs and squiggle into the saddle.

Satan scooted himself away from the fence to face Hilary, with her body draped over his back. She shrieked, remembering her terrifying dreams. Instead of dropping to the ground, Hilary instinctively swung her right leg over the saddle. As soon as she did, she regretted it. Satan, however, remained calm. He turned his head to observe the frightened girl, as if it had been his intention all along. Hilary broke out in silent laughter although she still quivered with fear. She had been scared out of her wits, and all Satan wanted was to see what she was doing.

The next morning was Sunday, Hilary's day off. She decided to get up early and ride Dolly before the heat settled in. On her way to the stables, she stopped and greeted Satan with a grin and an apple. Hearing voices coming from the barn, Hilary headed over to fetch Dolly and go for a ride.

She noticed a few kids getting ready for the Sunday lessons in the main barn as she headed to Dolly's field. When the old Appaloosa mare spotted Hilary, she lifted her head from grazing and ambled away. Hilary ran after her and clipped the lead rope to the halter. She decided to go on a soothing trail ride to relieve herself and her mount from the stress of yesterday's show.

As she rode along the earthen path, a voice interrupted the peace of the forest. "Hi there," it said, belonging to none other than Jeremy. He had just come down a nearby trail on Splash. He rode his horse beside Dolly. "I heard you did awesome in the farm show yesterday," he commented.

Hilary smiled weakly as they rode out into a field. "You must have heard wrong; I did horribly," she admitted, looking at Jeremy and laughing. "I got an honorable mention and a tenth place ribbon." Jeremy smiled, but for once, didn't laugh at her.

"You may think it's bad, but really, for your first show and all, it's pretty good," he replied. She shrugged. As they pushed their horses into a trot, Jeremy said, "You mind if I ride with you? Elise isn't coming back from Steven's farm until Tuesday."

"Sure, I don't mind at all," Hilary answered, surprised at his question. Since she came to Millbrooke Stables, she hadn't ridden with anyone. Sure, she followed a few kids on the trails once or twice, but she'd never had the pleasure of riding with a friend. Trying her best to look good, Hilary urged Dolly into a steady, rolling canter. Jeremy did the same, but looked about a million times better. *No, maybe two million*, Hilary thought.

The two teenagers rode for at least an hour before they stopped for lunch. They talked a lot about school and what subjects they preferred and excelled in. They told stories of experiences they'd had with not-so-favorable subjects and the teachers who taught them. Jeremy told Hilary how he learned to ride and all about the horse shows he'd attended. He said it was almost as though he were born on a horse. He rode all the time and was trained by not only his mom, but his dad, too. Hilary wondered if his father still rode; she'd never seen him around the barn.

As if reading her mind, Jeremy said to her, "My dad left when I was about five. He said he needed time to think his life over and decide if it was what he really wanted. My mom and I never saw him again."

Hilary saw the hurt look in his eyes, and not knowing what to say, walked along in silence for a while.

"So, I hear Elise is off training with some hot shot," she said, breaking the silence and waiting for details.

"Yeah, she and Lady are really good, you know. And Steven Myers, well, he's the top show jumper around, so where else would you send Elise? It was weird, though, because she wasn't even excited to go. I helped her load up, early Tuesday morning, and she acted as though it were just another day at the barn."

"How far away is Steven's place?" Hilary asked.

"That's the thing—he's about twelve hours from here so she should be thrilled at the chance to even go, you know? But hey, I don't understand girls anyway so..." he responded, trailing off at the end.

"Why is she going to train with him anyway? Is there some show? Your mom said something about that."

"Well, as I said, she and Lady are great at jumping, so they need a professional to prep them for the Championships, which are in a couple of months. First they went to a series of shows that qualified them for the big one, the East Coast Jumping Final. That's the one coming up and the others took place this spring," Jeremy said. "I've heard you can just skip the qualifiers and enter like it's a normal show. But all the good riders go to the qualifiers anyway, so they can prove to everyone how good they are. You should ask my mom more about it. It's all a little hazy to me."

Hilary felt a pang of jealousy. Deep down she envied Elise and wished she was the one training for some huge championship. She asked, "So, are you still thinking about taking Satan?"

"Are you kidding me? Of course not, there's no time. And even if there was, I'm all talk and no do, if you know what I mean. But sure, it'd be awesome to compete against some of those great junior jumpers, but it isn't really my dream." He paused. "It was more my mom's, and I just kind of went with the flow."

When Hilary and Jeremy returned to the stables they went to their different barns to unsaddle their mounts. "Come on, girl," coaxed Hilary, leading the drained horse to the wash stall at the end of the main barn. So much for an easy ride.

Hilary enjoyed spending time with Dolly. She liked riding, but she also loved the time she spent caring for the horses. She supposed Satan gave her that sense of happiness because he had improved so much under her training. He was the real reason she continued to ride and improve. She could picture a perfect image of her riding him in the East Coast Finals. *Oh how great it would be,* Hilary thought as she scraped the cool water off Dolly's coat to get all the sweat out.

When Hilary returned to her house around noon, her mother and father were just leaving. "Oh, there you are, honey. We figured you went to ride. In fact we were on our way to pick you up," Karen said, opening the car door and putting some bags in the front seat. "Your dad and I were about to head over to the neighbor's house just down the street. We've been planning for a couple weeks now to get together, but this is one of the first days your dad's had off. We kind of want you to come, dear. Brenda has a daughter, and I think she might be around your age. You'd probably have some fun."

"Sure, why not? I'll come," Hilary said, smiling. "I'll get changed." Hilary knew her parents were surprised at how easy-going she'd been lately. At her old home they would've been lucky to get her out of the house at all.

After riding in the car for a total of four minutes, the Thompson family pulled into a large driveway lined with immense poplar trees. In front of an average-sized house, a small swimming pool glistened in the summer's intense heat. *Sam would like that,* Hilary mused, knowing how much he liked to swim. A girl, who appeared to be her age, stepped out of the house and interrupted Hilary's thoughts. She was pretty, with short blonde hair, and bright green eyes. She walked to the car and waited for Hilary to open her door.

"Hi, I'm Amanda. I'm glad you came."

"Well, hello, Amanda. I'm Karen, this is my husband James, and here is Hilary, our daughter," Karen said. Hilary really disliked it when her mom introduced her to people. She had a mouth and could just as easily do it herself.

"Hey," Hilary said, instinctively rolling her eyes at Karen. Amanda saw and stifled a giggle. Hilary sensed that she and Amanda would become great friends.

Chapter Thirteen

"Come with me. I'll show you my room," Amanda said, leading the way through the house to a room lined with horse pictures. "Well, here it is."

"You ride?" Hilary asked, viewing the pictures that hung on the wall.

"Yeah, I ride at Millbrooke Stables."

Hilary laughed, "I ride there, too, Amanda. I have a summer job there as well."

"Really? I've never seen you there," Amanda said.

"Well, I've only been riding since school let out. And come to think of it, I haven't seen you either."

"Aha, mystery solved then. I just got back from vacationing with my mom and dad," Amanda explained, taking a seat on her bed and motioning for Hilary to do the same. "We went to France to visit my aunt and uncle for a few weeks. It was awesome. Have you traveled much?"

"No, I wish. I haven't been out of the United States. I consider myself lucky, though, because my friend, Joy, up in Delaware, has never set foot on a plane," Hilary said.

"You were good friends with Joy, weren't you?"

Hilary asked, "How did you know?"

"I can tell by the way you just said her name…as though you miss her. I bet it would be hard moving from the place you knew and grew up in," Amanda answered.

"Yeah, it was kind of hard, but I really like it here in Lewisburg, especially having the barn right next door to my house," Hilary said.

It was evening when Hilary finally left Amanda's house. They made plans to meet at the barn the next day and go on a trail ride. Amanda told Hilary about her horse, Silver Dollar. Silver was fresh off the track, meaning she was recently a race horse. Amanda was training her all by herself. She'd only owned the thoroughbred mare for two months, and still had a long wait before she would be able to show her, but she assured Hilary that Silver was well worth it.

When Hilary got home, she grabbed an apple and set out for Satan's pen. It was nearly dark so she figured it was safe to begin her training session. Thankfully, Karen and James didn't notice her leaving the house, for they were watching their favorite television show. *Perfect,* thought Hilary.

She gave Satan a decent grooming with the brushes she brought home a few days earlier. He sparkled before Hilary tacked him up. Then, just like the other night, she practiced leaning her body's weight on his back. Before long she sat in the saddle. She praised him and decided to take a few chances with her little mustang tonight. Hilary tightened the grip on her legs and clucked her tongue.

"Walk," she said. Satan hesitantly stepped forward. At the sound of Hilary's cheerful voice, he took another few steps, seeming to understand what she wanted, and continued to walk until told otherwise. There was no practical way to steer him though, so Hilary used the weight of her body by moving it to one side of the saddle and then the other. Astonishingly, the horse obeyed each command she gave him.

When Hilary dismounted and began untacking Satan she saw his ears drop and a sad look come over his eyes. Hilary, however, was bubbling with pride. *I trained that horse.*

"Hilary, over here!" called Amanda, trying to get her attention. Hilary looked around, squinting into the newly risen sun.

"Oh, hey! I didn't see you," Hilary called back, running over to the south barn where the boarders kept their horses.

"Ready to ride?" asked Amanda, smiling.

"Yeah, I was just grooming Dolly," Hilary answered. "Are you going to ride Silver?"

"No, no, she still can't go out of the ring. It would be way too overwhelming for her. I'm taking Carrousel, Susan's four-year-old. I helped her work him a lot last summer, so she lets me take him out on hacks now," Amanda explained. "I just had to clean Silver's stall."

"Hey, that's my job!" Hilary joked as each girl parted to tack up her mount.

They rode out to the prairie path, which led through a long field of corn. They didn't plan to stay out long but somehow lost track of time. They chatted as they took small canters and long trots. Hilary had begun to develop quite a good seat and was proud to show it off.

Amanda was a very good rider. Like Elise, she had a knack with horses, but a totally different style. Amanda allowed the horse to move underneath her instead of nagging at him the whole time. That was where she and Elise were different. Elise was a chore to be around, while Amanda was a charm.

When the two girls returned to the stables, it seemed as though they had known each other all their lives. Amanda helped Hilary do her chores. When finished, they decided to go swimming at Amanda's house. "We can walk to my house. It's not quite two miles," Amanda suggested, as Hilary followed her out of the east barn. As they walked along the side of the road Amanda asked, "Hey, Hil, do you know who that black horse is?"

"That's Satan. He arrived while you were away. He's Jeremy's, and everyone thinks he was abused."

"Where did they get him?" Amanda asked as she watched the horse from the road.

"Some lady named Mary. She didn't do anything to him—that was probably the previous owner. Apparently, she didn't have the guts to work with him, so she gave him to Susan. Then Susan gave him to Jeremy, because he's looking for a new horse."

"Splash is getting a bit old, I suppose."

"It's not that he's so old; it's that Jeremy's outgrown his abilities. At least that's what he told me." Hilary wondered whether she should tell Amanda about her training sessions with Satan. It was hard for her to keep something this important from Amanda, because it already seemed like they were best friends. She didn't have anyone to confide in, now that Joy and Ali weren't a big part of her life. Maybe she would call Joy tonight and tell her about Satan. But for now, she decided to keep her meetings with her mustang a secret from Amanda.

It was a beautiful night. The full moon hung low in the sky making everything easy to see. Hilary followed the training schedule she'd made by first grooming Satan. Next she began rubbing his back where he enjoyed being scratched. After a few minutes she placed the saddle on his back and tightened the girth. She tied the rope on both sides of his halter and led him over to the fence. Tonight, she didn't have to practice leaning on Satan, for he had become accustomed to her on his back.

"Good boy," Hilary said as the calm horse stepped obediently away from the fence and began walking around the paddock. Sometimes she would ask him to halt, then step back into a rhythmic walk. For the next five minutes she repeated this process until she felt sure Satan was ready to trot. She tightened her grip on the lead rope and squeezed slightly with her slender legs.

"Trot, boy." He walked faster then stepped into a two beat gait. Hilary giggled. *What a good boy he is!*

Suddenly Satan skidded to a halt and wheeled his muscular body around. He stampeded back to the far end of the paddock with Hilary hanging on. It was just like the dreams she had experienced. Thoughts whirled through her brain with a mixture of pictures and sounds. Could those dreams have forecast Hilary's future? Would Satan jump the fence? Would she fall? The terrifying thoughts vanished when she realized the horse had stopped.

Stunned that she was still alive, Hilary looked around. Yep, all was quiet, and Satan was still inside his corral. She glanced down at him. He looked very calm, but he stared suspiciously in the direction of the stables.

"It's all right, Satan. We're fine," she breathed, praying for her words to be true. She decided she really better dismount before the horse did something weird again. But just as she was swinging her leg over the saddle she stopped herself. If she dismounted, she might never ride Satan again for fear that her dreams were actually coming true. Thinking back to Susan's books on horse training Hilary remembered she must never end a ride on a bad note. So she settled herself back in the saddle. Still shaking slightly, she asked Satan to walk forward. He did as he was told, then backed up a few steps and raised his head. Hilary followed the startled horse's gaze and gasped, horrified at what she saw.

Chapter Fourteen

One of Hilary's worst nightmares had come true. Next to the fence at the far end of the paddock stood Jeremy. "Hilary, what on earth are you doing?" he yelled, climbing over the fence and walking slowly toward the horse. Hilary jumped off Satan just in time, as he went up on his two powerful hind legs and struck violently at the clear night's air.

"What the—!" Jeremy began, taken aback by the horse's sudden violence. Although Satan had been slightly agitated with Jeremy lurking in the shadows, it surprised Hilary when he reared up. She kept a tight grip on the rope and eased the horse back to the ground.

"Easy now, easy." Once Satan stood safely on his four legs, Hilary undid the girth and yanked the saddle off his back. She gave him a quick pat as he tore off to the other end of the paddock. Hilary wasn't any more thrilled about Jeremy's sudden appearance than the horse was. "You know better than to run up on a wild horse like that! I can't believe you."

"And I cannot believe you, Hilary!" Jeremy said, yelling now. "Who gave you the right to ride my horse, huh? Was it me? Was it my mom? No! You should've never touched Satan," Jeremy exclaimed, thrusting his arms into the air.

"For your information, Jeremy, I'm helping you," Hilary said, looking him in the eye and crossing her arms. "If it weren't for me this horse would still be unrideable."

"He *is* unrideable," Jeremy hollered back. "You're the only one who can ride him, so does that make him automatically broke?"

"Yes!" Hilary shouted, throwing *her* arms in the air.

"That was a rhetorical question, and the answer is no. You being the only one to ride, much less get near him, does not mean Satan is broke. Normal horses these days don't give a damn about who rides them," Jeremy sputtered before taking a deep breath.

"Well, some horses do, and Satan is one of them," Hilary added, once again crossing her arms.

"Let me tell you something, and listen very, very carefully," Jeremy began, pointing his index finger at Hilary. "You haven't been around horses your whole life; therefore, you don't know anything about them. Heck, you're not even a good rider!" Hilary was silent for a minute, before she finally spoke.

"You're right," she said simply, climbing out of the paddock and taking a seat under the old oak tree. "I mean, what good can reading every horse book in the world do for me if I don't have the experience like you and Elise and even Amanda?" Hilary asked as her eyes welled up with tears. Jeremy hopped over the fence and took a seat beside her under the tree.

•

"You've read all my Mom's books, and I think they really helped you."

Hilary couldn't hold back her tears any longer. "Helped me? So I really am a bad rider," she said, covering her face with her hands.

"No, no, you're not. I mean, I just said that...because...I don't know why. But you're not bad. It's true, you've only ridden for a short while, but you've already improved so much," Jeremy admitted, awkwardly pulling her hair back from her face. "Look, Hil," he said, tapping her shoulder. She glanced at Jeremy's distressed face and felt her frown disappear. He was trying so hard to comfort her but just didn't know how. "Listen, the real reason I'm so mad is because...because I'm jealous of you," he finished, looking relieved to get it out. He continued when Hilary had nothing to say. "I just wish it was me, you know, riding Satan. You trained him and I admit he is a trained horse now," he said. Hilary's frowning mouth relaxed slightly, and she looked up into Jeremy's eyes.

"You really mean that?"

"Yeah, I do. And you want me to let you in on a little something?" Jeremy asked, not waiting for a reply. "My mom said last night that if I cannot train Satan in a week, he'll go back to Mary."

Hilary's jaw tightened, and she sat up straighter against the tree. "Well, what are you going to do?"

"You know, Hil, if you help me train this horse, since you're the only one he trusts, my Mom will let us keep him," he said. "So...?" he prompted.

"So, I don't know," Hilary pouted.

"What do you mean you don't know?" Jeremy exclaimed. "Then we can both ride him all the time."

"You mean you'll get to ride him all the time," she corrected. "Why should I help you if there's nothing in it for me?" She wasn't a greedy person, but this was a big deal. She loved Satan and wished he was her own.

Jeremy was quiet for a moment. "If you don't help me, I'll tell my mom what you've been doing, and she'll kick you out of the stables," Jeremy told Hilary. If she didn't comply with Jeremy's plan, Satan would go back to Mary, and then who knows where he'd end up. Hilary couldn't let that happen.

"I guess I have no choice, do I?" Hilary mumbled with a surly stare at Jeremy. Jeremy shook his head and looked over at Satan.

"So, you're the training expert now," he complimented her, somewhat jokingly. "Where do we begin?"

"We won't be doing anything tonight. Satan's tired. But first I need to get some things straight," Hilary said, thinking carefully. "You won't tell Susan if I help Satan learn to trust you?"

"And train," Jeremy corrected, nodding his head.

"Yeah, whatever. So that's it then, nothing more?"

"Well, sort of," Jeremy said, straining his neck out like a turtle. "You see, you can't tell anyone you helped me train him. We're going to pretend it was all me—who trained him, I mean."

"What! Are you kidding? Not only do I have to help

you train a horse I can never ride, but I can't even take credit for it?" Hilary spluttered, unable to believe her ears. The deal sucked. She was proud of herself for the work she'd done with him, and it was hard enough already that she couldn't tell Susan. She knew she'd probably be kicked out of the barn, but wouldn't Susan be a little proud of her?

"I know it's not fair, but there's no other way. Come on, Hilary, please?" Jeremy pleaded.

"Fine, but I can't believe I'm doing this for you," she murmured, scarcely loud enough for him to hear.

"Wahoo! I knew you'd agree, Hil!" Jeremy whooped, smiling broadly. "Just think; wouldn't it be ironic if I actually get to the Championships on Satan? And imagine if I beat Elise! Ha-ha, that would be a funny sight. Can you imagine the look on her face?"

Hilary rolled her eyes in disgust. She grabbed her saddle and turned toward the house.

"Hey, where are you going? Aren't we going to make up a secret schedule on when we're going to train?" Jeremy asked, jumping up and running after Hilary.

"We'll do that tomorrow," she said flatly.

"Well, at least let me give you my number," Jeremy said, grabbing a pad of paper Hilary had used to write out Satan's training schedule and running after her. "In case we ever have to coordinate a time to meet."

Hilary snatched the paper from Jeremy and left the boy standing at her front door.

Chapter Fifteen

"Sorry I was kind of a drag today, Hil," Amanda apologized, "I'm just not that into shopping."

Earlier that morning the two girls had gone on another relaxing hack in the woods. After riding, Amanda helped Hilary with her daily chores. When they were finished, Karen had picked them up, Hilary practically dragging Amanda behind her, and headed for the mall. Surprisingly, it was almost as big as the Christiana, back in Delaware.

It was Hilary's first time shopping since she had moved, and she couldn't wait to set her foot in American Eagle. "Amanda, you have to come with me; it'll be so much fun!" she'd pleaded earlier that morning.

But for some reason, once Hilary started browsing her favorite stores, she found herself not as enthralled as she once had been. No longer did she feel the need to try on every pair of jeans. Nor did she snatch a skirt while strolling by a display and say, "Do you think this would look good on me?" Shopping used to be fun with Ali and Joy, but on that particular day, Hilary found she'd rather be back at Millbrooke with the horses.

The one catch Karen had bestowed upon them was that they take Sam along and help him buy some new clothes. Hilary had grudgingly agreed, and to her astonishment, she didn't mind Sam's company. She and Amanda took him to the stores he wanted to visit, and Hilary even bought him an ice cream cone. Was she becoming a softie for her brother? Lately, she and Sam hadn't gotten into a single argument.

In the lounge that morning, before Hilary went riding with Amanda, she and Jeremy had put together their training schedule for Satan. Every morning at five they would meet in his paddock. They would begin the first few sessions by letting Jeremy earn Satan's trust. "Trust is the first thing a horse and rider must develop," Hilary had told him. "If you don't have that, you don't have anything. After a couple of days when I'm certain you two trust each other, we'll progress to the hands-on work. I will allow you to groom him and rub his favorite spots, but that's it," she'd explained, feeling rather superior as head trainer. "After two days of that I will allow you to tack him up, but not ride him. Then you'll easily be able to sit on him, and before we know it, you'll be popping over cross rails." Jeremy said he didn't have any objections to Hilary's timeline of training, but he made it quite clear that he wanted to ride his horse soon.

Hilary met Jeremy in Satan's corral at precisely five the next morning. It was cool, and the birds were just beginning their morning rituals. First Hilary greeted Satan with the usual apple and a pat. She spent a few minutes soothing the horse, who was already worked up with Jeremy watching from the fence. When she felt he was comfortable, she walked toward the fence where their observer stood. Satan followed her a few yards then put his head up in the air, ears alert, and blew a nervous snort, his eyes on Jeremy.

"Easy, it's just Jer, boy," she said, walking back to him. Hilary realized she would have to move gradually to get him accustomed to Jeremy's presence.

After a quick hour, Hilary and Jeremy walked off to the stables to begin some chores. They were both slightly disappointed that Satan had maintained his distance from Jeremy the whole session, refusing to focus, even when Hilary tried to calm him.

"He just hates other people," Hilary said, confused. "I thought, now that he's trained and everything, he wouldn't mind. I mean, I know he'll learn to love you one day, but how long will it take? We haven't got months if you still want to go to the champs."

"I really would like to go. Have you seen the legs on that horse? He looks like he could jump the moon," Jeremy added as they entered the east barn.

"He jumps like he could jump the moon, too. I saw him jump out that one night and..." Hilary paused and looked over at Jeremy. "I saw what I saw, and I know you think I'm insane."

"No, you're not insane. I'll admit it now that we're training him together. It's true, he did jump out—but you can't tell my mom," he added hurriedly.

"Okay, I won't. But how did he get back in?"

"I was so lucky. See, I was trying to do one of those join-up things, and he got scared and started running around the paddock. Then he just jumped out. I ran and opened the gate so I could try to herd him back in. Before I knew it, a car came blazing down the street and spooked him, and he galloped back into the corral. As I said, it was the luckiest thing that's ever happened to me." Jeremy laughed just thinking about it. "I was so scared he was going to get hit by that car. Imagine what my mom would have said."

"Wow!" Hilary grabbed a pitch fork and began cleaning Lotto's stall. What if Satan really had run out into the road? Hilary's life would be so different. She hoped nothing like that would ever happen to Satan.

"Well, I'll see you tomorrow morning. I'm going to a football game tonight in town," Jeremy said, patting Splash and heading out of the barn.

Hilary and Jeremy were dismayed at the little progress Satan made during the week. Although he no longer quivered when Jeremy stood near him, he still hadn't accepted the boy petting him. Both teens were certain he would improve, but it hadn't happened so far, and now it was getting late.

"All right, Jeremy, let's see you handle Satan," Susan said as she stood up from a chair in the lounge one Saturday morning. "I've wanted to see you work with him, but I've just been too busy with everything around here."

Hilary and Jeremy exchanged horror-struck looks. What were they going to do?

"Yeah, sure, Mom," Jeremy said, eyeing Hilary.

Hilary knew Jeremy had been fibbing to his mom about Satan's progress. What would Susan do when she realized her son had been dishonest? "I have an idea," she whispered through clenched teeth as she and Jeremy headed toward Satan's field. "Leave it to me."

As the three of them neared the paddock, a few lesson kids trailed behind, eager to watch the black horse in a session. Hilary and Jeremy sank back in the line while she murmured her plan to him. He nodded in agreement. By the time they reached the fence, it was all settled.

"And since I have trained him so well, I'll even let Hilary show you how docile he is," Jeremy said as the group of observers settled by the fence. "Not only is he perfect with me, but he'll let other people handle him. I think that's saying something about how well I trained him."

Hilary slipped through the fence and went over to Satan, who looked wary on the other side of the paddock. She prayed for everything to go smoothly and hoped he wasn't startled by the crowd.

"Hey," she said, patting him on the neck. Susan smiled and hugged Jeremy beside her, murmuring what a fabulous job he had done.

"There's more, Mom, look," he said in an effort to stop Susan from strangling him. His mom smiled again as Hilary picked up each hoof and then led him around the far end of the paddock.

"You've done a fantastic job, Jer," Susan said. Hearing a door slam, she turned around. "Oh, look, Elise is back! Keep up the good work!" Susan and the rest of the students hurried over to the main barn to welcome Lady and Elise home. Hilary and Jeremy each let out a long breath.

"Thanks, Hil, that was a close one," Jeremy smiled, leaving Hilary and following the others. Hilary stroked Satan and fed him a sugar cube. Maybe he really had improved, for he hadn't seemed too bothered by all the people who had watched him. Hilary smiled to herself as she headed over to greet Elise.

That night Hilary rode Satan. Using her saddle, she walked and trotted around the corral, praising him every few steps. She couldn't believe what a fast learner he was. Even if he had done all of this before, Hilary had started from square one after whatever had gone wrong with his previous rider. And just a week earlier, she had only been leaning a little of her weight on his back. Now look what they were doing!

When she was finished, she went inside to call Amanda. The two of them had planned a sleep-over, and Hilary had forgotten all about it until now.

"Hello?" Amanda answered in a cheery voice.

"Amanda, it's me."

"Hil, I was wondering when you'd call!"

"Yeah, sorry, I was still outside," Hilary said, leaving it at that.

"That's okay. So are we still on for tonight?"

"I am if you are. My mom says it's fine."

"Great, I'll see you in five minutes or so?"

"Sure, see you then," Hilary finished, hanging up the phone. *Oh no!* She thought, *I forgot all about Jeremy!*

Immediately, Hilary picked up the phone and dialed his number. She explained that she and Amanda had planned a sleepover, and therefore, she would be unable to work with him and Satan the next morning.

"I really wish I could tell her though. It's so hard to keep a secret from a good friend. I don't think she'd pass it on if I did tell her," Hilary said to Jeremy.

"No, you can't tell anyone, and neither can I, okay?"

"Fine, fine. So I'll see you tomorrow night then?"

"Yeah, I'll probably see you at the barn first though," he said. Hilary heard a knock at the door downstairs.

"Listen I have to run—I'll see you sometime tomorrow." She heard a click at the other end of the line and went running downstairs to let Amanda in. Sam had already done so, however, and was questioning Amanda in the living room.

"Hey, Amanda, sorry about him." Hilary pointed to Sam. "He gets excited when I have friends over."

The girls went up to Hilary's room and chatted enthusiastically about the horses and people of Millbrooke as they listened to music and played a board game. They each won two games but got sick of playing and neglected a tie-breaker. Deep into the night, they continued chatting in hushed voices.

It was surprising to Hilary that she and Amanda had

already become such good friends. Back in Delaware, Hilary wouldn't have associated with a girl who was crazy about horses and didn't like shopping. Everything was changing in her life, and Hilary admitted to herself that it was for the better.

Chapter Sixteen

Hilary and Amanda had an early breakfast and headed to the barn to ride Amanda's horse, Silver. As
they passed Satan's paddock the horse gave a high pitched
whinny and trotted over to Hilary.

"Run!" Hilary shouted, pulling Amanda by the arm
and leaping forward. "He does that to me every day," she
explained when they reached the main barn. "I'm telling you now, that horse is C-R-A-Z-Y," she spelled out as
Amanda laughed at her.

"Everyone thinks he's so frightening, but he reminds
me of a normal untamed horse," Amanda commented as
the two headed to the south barn.

"But he looks mean," defended Hilary, snapping her
teeth teasingly at Amanda.

"I guess so. When are they going to start training him,
anyway?" she asked. Hilary realized that Amanda must
not have heard about the presentation she and Jeremy had
given to everyone the other day.

"Jeremy's already working with him," Hilary told her,
determined not to say any more about it.

When they reached the South Barn, Amanda explained every procedure she did with Silver. She even showed Hilary how to tell a horse's age by their teeth.

"You have to observe the way the incisors are angled and whether they have a Galvan's groove—a small dent on the horses' side tooth that runs from the top of it down," she said, running her finger along Silver's tooth.

"If the groove is clearly noticeable at the top of the tooth, the horse is around ten or eleven. If it is half way down, the horse is somewhere around fifteen, and if it goes all the way down, they're twenty. If there's no groove the horse is either older than twenty-five or younger than eleven," she finished patting Silver. "And a horse is said to have a 'full mouth' at age five, when they get all of their teeth." Hilary felt an urge to look at Satan's mouth right then. She had always wondered how old he was, but she knew it would have to wait.

Amanda longed Silver in the outdoor ring and allowed Hilary to try as well. The horse moved on a rope around where she stood in the center of the circle. When they decided the gray mare had had enough longing for one day, Amanda asked if Hilary would mind leading her around the ring atop Silver. Hilary gladly helped her friend, and when they were finished, the two girls chatted excitedly about Silver's progress.

Hilary wanted to tell Amanda of her own training sessions, but she couldn't. Not yet—soon, but not yet.

When they finished with Amanda's horse, the thirsty trainers headed to the lounge for a cold drink.

"Oh, would you look who the cat dragged in," spoke a cold voice belonging to no other than Elise.

"Hey, Elise, how did your working student program go with Steven?" Amanda asked cheerfully.

How could Amanda be so pleasant when Elise was so rude?

"Actually, Amanda, I wasn't a working student because I didn't work for him. I was specifically there to become a better rider than I already was, and I think I've accomplished that," boasted Elise.

Amanda smiled and sat down with Hilary on the couch. "That's great. It sounds like you'll do really well at the finals," she said.

Elise strode over to Jeremy, who had just come through the door. She greeted him with a kiss on the lips which made Hilary cringe with disgust. Amanda was saying something but Hilary was a too distracted to hear.

Didn't Jeremy realize what Elise was really like? Why did he like her so much? *She may be a great rider, but she's not a great person,* thought Hilary. She had been looking forward to meeting with him that evening. But after watching Elise all over him, Hilary's ideas changed. Would it start to get awkward between them now that Elise was back?

That night Hilary lay under the big oak as Jeremy handled Satan in the corral. Fireflies appeared here and there, and hoot owls called to one another from the trees.

Hilary fixed her attention on the boy standing beside his mustang, coaxing him to eat an apple.

In the light of the moon, Hilary watched Satan's eye following Jeremy warily. She wanted to comfort Satan— to let him know that everything would be okay—but she didn't. Hilary knew she shouldn't interfere for Jeremy's sake, but even more importantly, for Satan's. On behalf of the horse's future, she couldn't mess this up. This was possibly the last chance Jeremy would have to earn Satan's trust before his mom would want to see him handle the horse himself. *And if Susan realizes Satan is afraid of Jeremy she'll have no choice but to send him off.*

Early the next morning, at Hilary's usual meeting time with Jeremy, she dragged herself out of bed and got dressed. She headed outside, still groggy, but was immediately aroused by what she saw. In the corral stood Jeremy, lifting up one of Satan's legs. When he finished with that one, he stroked the horse and moved on to another. Hilary smiled happily and ran over to them.

"Jer! That's wonderful," she exclaimed, as Satan pulled away from Jeremy and trotted over to her.

Jeremy smiled back, "Yeah, I've been out here since three. I used a lot of grain to lure him to me, but he finally let me pet him."

"That's great. You can pet him everywhere?" Hilary asked while Satan rubbed his head on her shoulder.

"Just about; he doesn't like it when I touch his face."

"Well, then, let's get to work," Hilary said, snapping a lead on Satan's halter and leading him toward the middle of the paddock.

Hilary took a few minutes to stroke his head with her own gentle hand. Then she took Jeremy's hand in hers and rubbed it on Satan's face. The now gentle horse seemed to think it was still Hilary petting him, for he did not pull away. After a few minutes Hilary told Jeremy to keep rubbing while she pulled her own hand out from underneath his. Noticing that it was clearly Jeremy petting him, Satan quivered but didn't move. Jeremy praised him and took his hand away.

When Satan seemed comfortable with Jeremy's touch, Hilary mentioned what Amanda had said about a horse's teeth. "Yeah, it's true," Jeremy responded, forcing his thumb into Satan's mouth and causing the horse to give in. He squinted, looking Satan's teeth up and down. "He looks to be five or six," he said.

By the end of their training session Hilary was feeling slightly put out. No longer was she the only person to groom Satan. Jeremy had successfully brushed him and even got him to open his mouth—something even she hadn't done. They agreed to meet early the next morning to work on tacking him up.

Hilary had a lesson with Susan that day and jumped her first cross rail. Dolly was well behaved and, as always, took care of her rider. However, through the entire lesson Hilary pretended that the horse, so mannerly and strong between her legs, was not Dolly, but Satan. She felt guilty in doing so; Dolly was a made horse, she was completely trained and uncomplicated to ride. But maybe that was just it. Hilary hadn't been the one to train Dolly, and she wasn't the mare's only rider. Satan, however, was like a piece of her. He seemed to understand her. Whenever she would walk by his paddock, he would greet her with a whinny and a kiss. Dolly, on the other hand, wouldn't even lift her head when Hilary spoke to her.

Nevertheless, when the lesson was over, Hilary was feeling pleased. Even if she hadn't been riding her beautiful Satan, she had learned how to jump, *and that's a great accomplishment,* she thought.

Afterwards, she helped Amanda with Silver. When they finished, Amanda's mom treated them to an ice cream at a restaurant downtown. By the time evening arrived, Hilary was exhausted. She dreaded waking up at the crack of dawn to help Jeremy with Satan. *If only our training sessions didn't have to be so secretive,* she thought.

"Just a few more minutes," Hilary groaned when her alarm clock defeated the silence of the morning. With great effort she dragged herself from bed. When she walked outside, she noticed Jeremy had already tacked the horse.

"Sorry I'm late; I was really tired," she said. Jeremy didn't seem to hear her, and if he did, he didn't respond.

"I'm going to ride him today," he finally announced.

"Are you sure?" Hilary questioned, suddenly feeling uneasy. "What if you get hurt?"

"Then I get hurt, and I try again. He looks pretty calm, doesn't he?" Jeremy said, patting Satan's velvety nose.

He did—it was true, but Satan still wasn't as comfortable with Jeremy as he was with Hilary. You could see it in his eyes, but he accepted Jeremy's presence. He allowed Jeremy to do everything Hilary did, so maybe it was time for the boy to ride his horse. Even if it wasn't, Jeremy convinced her to assist him. Still, she was uncomfortable with the idea.

"Why don't you hop on him first and ride him around a little," Jeremy suggested. Hilary nodded and swung her leg over the saddle. That was Jeremy's best idea all week.

After Hilary walked, trotted, and even tried a little canter she pulled him up to a halt and dismounted.

"Here I go," said Jeremy, climbing the fence and reaching for the saddle.

When Satan saw Jeremy's hand reaching out, he stepped away from the fence. Jeremy tumbled to the ground. Hilary clamped her hand over her mouth, trying to conceal her laughter. Jeremy lay, face first, in a pile of muck and sputtered to dislodge the dirt from his mouth. *Even Satan looks amused,* Hilary thought.

Turning over and dusting off his pants, Jeremy, too, broke out in hysterical laughter after seeing Hilary's suppressed giggles. When they got control of themselves, he tried to mount Satan again. Hilary, keeping a tighter grip on the horse's halter this time, persuaded him to hold still. Once Jeremy was all set, she let go.

"I guess I'll just walk around the paddock for a while,"

Jeremy said to Hilary. But Satan had different ideas. When Jeremy squeezed his sides, ever so gently, the sleek horse leapt violently into the air. Jeremy, being a very good rider, hung on with all he had. The suddenness of Satan's brutal leap, however, dislodged him slightly, and no matter how hard he clung to the saddle, he was slipping. After another ferocious buck, Jeremy hit the hard ground with a thump. He managed to land on his feet, and somehow, he still held the lead rope.

"Are you okay?" Hilary asked, horrified at what had just happened. Jeremy nodded, smiled, and wiped his forehead. He led Satan to the fence and retrieved his hard hat, which he had refused to wear before.

"I guess I'll put this on now," he said, buckling it under his chin and walking back to the distressed horse.

"No, Jeremy, don't ride him again! You'll get hurt," Hilary protested. But he ignored her objection and told her to lead Satan back to the fence.

After what had just happened, the horse was foaming with sweat and refused to let Jeremy near him again. It took Hilary a few minutes to calm him, and following Jeremy's orders, she led him back to the fence. This time Jeremy was determined not to fall and, once again, asked the animal to walk. Satan stepped daintily forward but soon came to a halt, confused. He was obviously frightened of Jeremy; the whites of his eyes were exposed and his nostrils flared.

"Walk on!" Jeremy said, determined to get his way.

With the sudden order from his rider, Satan backed

up, his tail clenched to his rump. His haunches shook. He slammed into the fence, the sudden collision startling him and making him hurtle forward.

Hilary closed her eyes and prayed for both horse and rider to remain unharmed. "Jer, get off of him!" she shrieked, as tears began to stream from her eyes. She couldn't stand to see Jeremy get hurt, and she couldn't bear the agony her Satan was going through.

Jeremy ignored Hilary as he fought to bring Satan to a halt. He had no such luck. Each time the horse catapulted into the air, Jeremy became a little less balanced.

"Jeremy, do an emergency dismount!" Hilary screamed, terrified as the horse and rider launched into the air again. Jeremy appeared as though he heard Hilary's order that time, for he tried to slide his leg over the saddle. But Satan was going too fast, and Jeremy seemed too unnerved to jump off.

After a long battle between horse and rider, Satan, now completely lathered, his nostrils trickling blood and his hindquarters quivering, reared up. Hilary watched both horse and rider tumble over backwards, as if in slow motion, ending in a deafening crash. Hilary screamed and ran to the motionless pair.

Chapter
Seventeen

"Jeremy, wake up!" Hilary cried, grabbing his shoulders and pulling until his legs slid out from under Satan's side. "Jeremy, wake up!"

Hilary was afraid to look at Satan. She prayed for him not to be dead, but she knew she had to concentrate on Jeremy now. She pressed her ear to his chest and heard a very slow heartbeat. She had to get an ambulance.

Hilary ran to her house and grabbed the phone. With shaking fingers, she dialed 911 before running upstairs to wake her mom. James had been on shift at the hospital since early that morning, so there was no doctor nearby.

"Mom! Mom, wake up. Jeremy's hurt!"

With wide, glazed eyes, Karen bolted from the bed.

"What?" she asked.

"Hurry! It's bad!" Hilary begged.

Hilary made sure her mom was following and ran for the door. She stopped while Karen grabbed a blanket and something from the freezer then led the way. When they came in view of Jeremy lying motionless in the middle of the pasture, Karen sprinted ahead.

Hilary saw Satan standing in the corner, shaking with fear. She wanted to go comfort him but knew she had to help Jeremy first. The boy remained still for a few moments, then groggily opened his eyes.

"Jeremy, honey, how many fingers?" Karen pleaded, while placing an icepack on his head.

"Four," he replied. Karen murmured something and asked him what hurt.

"My leg," he moaned.

"Hil, stay with him. I'm going to get Susan," Karen whispered. She ran like a gazelle for Susan's house, which rested in the rolling hills on the far side of the property.

"Jeremy, I'm so sorry," Hilary said through tears, tucking the blanket under his chin. "This is all my fault."

Hilary lay beside Jeremy for the next few minutes, trying her best to stay calm. She cried silently, wishing she could turn back time. After what seemed like ages, the piercing sound of sirens filled the quiet morning. When the ambulance finally pulled up into the Thompson's driveway, three men jumped out with a stretcher. They were putting Jeremy in the back of the ambulance when Susan and Karen arrived at the scene.

"Jeremy!" Susan cried as she climbed in beside her son. Two of the men hopped into the front of the truck while the third leapt into the back with Susan. The ambulance sped away, leaving Karen and Hilary huddled in the drive.

Hilary shakily and reluctantly told her mom what had happened, glancing over at Satan every few seconds. She told about the horse rearing over backwards with Jeremy. That was really all there was to tell.

"But why so early?" Karen pleaded, looking deep into her daughter's eyes. Hilary couldn't take this any longer. No one would understand her situation. As her eyes welled up with more tears, she fumbled for a response, her lower lip shuddering. After a moment she turned and fled for the safety of the corral.

When Hilary reached Satan, he shied away from her. "It's me, boy," she cried, slowly walking toward him, her hand outstretched. "It's Hilary."

After a minute, she stood by his side and slid the saddle off his back, placing it on the ground beside them. Under the cotton saddle pad, foamy sweat outlined the place where the saddle had been. Satan lowered his head as Hilary moved on to the halter and slid the leather piece over his ears. Then, as though a magnet had pulled them together, she let go of all her tension and wrapped her arms around Satan's neck, her fingers entwined in his mane. He responded immediately and pressed his warm muzzle into her back, holding Hilary close to his body.

After filling a bucket with warm water from the house and sponging off Satan's body, Hilary rubbed his legs with cool water until she was sure he would be okay. Satan, glued to Hilary's side, followed her to the fence, where she slipped through and headed for her house.

"Jeremy has sustained an undisplaced fracture of his left tibia. He will need to wear a cast for at least eight weeks.

He's a lucky young man. It could have been much worse," the doctor explained to Susan, Karen, and Hilary later that morning. He continued speaking in what Hilary believed was a different language—doctor language.

When they released Jeremy from the emergency room, he looked exhausted and collapsed into Karen's car, stiffly placing his crutches in the back and sagging into the comfort of the seat. He and Hilary avoided eye contact as much as possible until Jeremy abruptly broke the silence.

"It wasn't your fault," he mumbled, as though he were speaking to the window, avoiding Hilary's stare. She turned to look at him and mouthed the words, "Yes, it was," and returned to staring out her own window.

When she returned home, Hilary crawled into bed and gratefully closed her eyes. The next thing she knew, it was late afternoon. She hadn't meant to go to sleep. She quickly dressed and went over to the barn to carry out her chores. Amanda asked her millions of questions about where she had been and whether she was okay. Hilary could tell her friend was worried about her, but she never let the truth slip out of her mouth. She didn't see Jeremy, but word had gotten out about his accident. Apparently he had already told everyone what had happened. Hilary wondered how much he had told them. Why should she keep a secret she's dying to tell, if he wouldn't keep it himself?

The next few days went by in a haze. It was almost as though Jeremy had disappeared off the face of the earth. Hilary had gone over to his house on Friday and Saturday, but he never answered the door. She knew he was in there but figured he was too embarrassed to face her. Really, there wasn't much to be ashamed of in Hilary's point of view. So why wouldn't he talk to her? She had even tried calling him on Sunday. He answered the phone dully, but when he heard Hilary's voice he said, "Oh, I have something to do. Got to go."

Hilary was furious. She slammed the phone back into the receiver and ripped up a post-it-note she had lying on her desk. Jeremy was starting to go a little too far with this game of his.

On Monday morning, she was determined to locate him and figure out what was bothering him. She went to his house, the East Barn, the arenas, and finally the lounge. There he was with Elise on his lap, talking and laughing with a few of his friends. Hilary couldn't believe it! Here she was terribly worried, while Jeremy's having the time of his life.

"Jeremy, get over here," she ordered, stomping her foot impatiently. "We need to talk."

Everyone laughed at Hilary's remark, and although Jeremy suddenly stiffened, he laughed as well.

"Go away, Hilary. We don't have time for kids," he joked rudely, ignoring her and resuming his chatter. Hilary couldn't believe her ears. She bit back an angry retort. After all she'd done for him, this was how he repaid her? She'd endured this long enough.

"Come with me now, or I'll tell them," she threatened. Jeremy's friends stopped laughing. They gaped as he grudgingly pushed Elise away and walked out the door.

"What?" he yelled, hobbling away from the publicity of the barn as fast as he could on his new crutches.

"I just need to talk to you, okay?" Hilary pleaded.

"There's not much to talk about."

Hilary was shocked. "Yes there is! You and Satan and all of that."

"What about it, Hilary? If you're here to make fun of me, you can forget it, all right? I knew I could never befriend that horse in the first place, so you don't need to tell me how stupid it was of me to think I could," Jeremy spat. "Satan will never trust anyone but you. I thought I could make it work, but I was wrong."

Hilary took in a deep breath and continued.

"Look, I think we're both a little flustered by the whole thing, so let's just take a minute to think about it, okay?

"No, just go back to whatever you were doing, and I'll go back to what I was doing." Jeremy replied heatedly, gripping his crutches and heading back to the lounge.

Hilary watched him go and felt a lump swell up in her throat. She wished he would stop taking things out on her. She'd put so much effort into helping him with Satan, sacrificing her own relationship with the horse, and now this?

That evening Hilary went to visit Satan. She knew he must be confused because she hadn't been out to see him lately. He nickered excitedly at her.

She twirled her tired hands in his mane and let her tears flow. She felt terrible for the mustang. She wished everything was the way it used to be—just her and Satan riding alone in the paddock without Jeremy to ruin their special twosome. Trying not to reattach herself to the unique animal, she turned and fled for home.

To Hilary's surprise, there was an envelope addressed to her, on the front door of the house. She grabbed it and ran upstairs to her room. Slowly she read:

Hilary,
I've been a real jerk, and I know it. I'm not afraid to tell you that. The things I said were thoughtless, and I appreciate all the work you put into Satan and me. My mom doesn't want me to ride him anymore after what happened, so she's selling him. I don't know what will happen to him, but I really do care. I hope he gets a good home with whoever buys him.
                    Jer
P.S. We're taking him to the Lewisburg horse auction tomorrow, and my mom wants you to help her load him into the trailer.
P.P.S. I told her you're the only one he really trusts.

Hilary set the letter down and held back her tears. She had to remain strong for Satan. She couldn't believe he was to go to an auction. Everyone was going to underestimate a horse like Satan. If no one could touch him or even get near him, how would he get a home? Then she realized that was just it; she'd answered her own question. He wouldn't get a home. He would be sent to the slaughterhouse. She grabbed Jeremy's letter, ripped it in half, and watched it flutter to the floor. She stood up and sighed deeply, then ran from her room, which was no longer a comfort to her. She needed to be with Satan and have one last ride. She grabbed her tack and headed outside into the dark night.

Hilary experienced the best ride she'd ever had on her powerful little stallion. It was almost as though he felt his passenger's sadness. He performed like a horse that'd been under saddle all his life. He never set one hoof out of place. She even cantered. And not just a little canter—a big canter. The two frolicked around the paddock for what seemed like an eternity until Satan seemed to sense Hilary's tiredness and came to a halt.

She would never forget this horse.

Chapter Eighteen

The morning sun was hidden by a thick layer of clouds. Hilary slouched against the oak near Satan's paddock, wishing everything would go back to the way it used to be. But things never would, because today Satan would be leaving. Hilary had spent all morning with him, and looking at her watch, she knew her time was up. She trudged to Millbrooke. Scanning the parking lot for the trailer that would take Satan to his demise, she found it still unattached to the truck. She looked around and realized that the farm was vacant. *Where is everybo…*

"SURPRISE!" yelled a flock of people descending on her from the barn. Hilary was stunned. It wasn't her birthday—of that she was positive. But what else could it be?

"Hilary," Susan began, "Jeremy told me all about you and Satan; how you worked with him and tried to help him form a bond with the horse. He explained all about the relationship you and Satan have and…" her voice broke. "I despise taking horses to auctions, so I'm following Jer's orders, and I truly believe it's the right thing to do—I'm going to give Satan one more chance. But not with my son—with you, Hilary. Jeremy thinks you deserve to have Satan as your own." As Susan finished, everyone began to whoop and cheer.

Just then a limping Jeremy led a dark-colored horse from the other side of the barn to meet Hilary in the parking lot. There was no doubt that the horse was Satan for he pranced nervously beside Jeremy. When he saw Hilary he whinnied and pulled away from his handler. He trotted up to her.

She threw her arms around his neck, and tears of joy trickled from her misty eyes. This was what she'd dreamt of for so long—Satan as her own horse and the promise of the East Coast Championships. All of her dreams suddenly fit into place. It was like the missing piece on a jigsaw puzzle finally being discovered. It was the perfect fairy-tale ending—but for her and Satan, it was really just the beginning.

"Congratulations," Elise said, as Amanda and Hilary walked past the arena in which Elise was riding. "On your first pony, that is. I'm certain you'll have oodles of fun riding around in circles." She smirked as she brought Lady to a halt and dismounted.

Although Elise was trying to bring Hilary down, she surely wasn't succeeding. Earlier that morning, Satan had become Hilary's, and there was nothing anyone could say that would dampen her spirits. Susan had helped Hilary move Satan into the boarders' barn. She would have to pay a monthly bill for the stall, but with all the work she'd been doing lately, money wouldn't be a problem. Satan settled in remarkably well, considering he had rarely set foot out of the corral by Hilary's house.

Hilary bedded the stall thickly, and just as she used to do, she read a book to her horse. Satan seemed to enjoy his stable mate, Silver, who happily munched hay from across the aisle. Since Satan was a stallion, the only stall safe enough to hold him was the one between the feed and tack stalls. This way he wouldn't get riled up by touching noses with other horses.

Once Hilary was sure his water was fresh and he was managing without her, she had walked over to Amanda's house to go swimming. In the late afternoon, the two of them strolled back to the south barn.

"Hilary? Why didn't you tell me you were training Satan?" Amanda asked as they slipped inside the barn, careful not to let the cool air escape. The way she asked, Hilary knew it had been bothering her for some time. She gulped, realizing she couldn't justify her secretiveness—except for maybe one thing.

"At first I guess I just didn't want you to put me down. I was kind of worried you'd laugh at me if I told you I was trying to break a mustang," Hilary admitted, glancing at her friend's intent expression, "and then when Jeremy asked me to help him train Satan, he made me swear to keep it a secret."

"But you know I'd never have told anyone, Hilary. Don't you?" asked Amanda, sounding earnest, but hurt.

"Yeah, I mean, I definitely know…now."

"But you didn't then, I guess?" Amanda said, filling in the blanks for her friend.

Hilary nodded, as she went into the large box stall to groom her new horse. "I always wanted to tell you," she said. "I should've known you wouldn't laugh at me."

The next morning Hilary met Amanda at the barn for a short ride. She wasn't sure how Satan would react, but she hoped to walk and trot in the outdoor arena. Come to think of it, this was a whole new life for Satan. Since he'd come to Millbrooke, he had never set foot outside the small corral near Hilary's, except of course when he jumped the fence.

"He might be excitable after being inside last night," Amanda pointed out as she led Silver into the ring. As Hilary followed, leading a wary Satan, she had to agree. He wasn't used to being cooped up. Nor was he used to a bridle, which Hilary had just put on him, but so far, he was being perfect with it. Hilary rode him to the rail. She walked around the arena a few times before beginning some walk-halt transitions. The two girls could hardly believe how placid he was, considering the numerous students running around in the main barn.

Once Hilary was confident all would go well, she squeezed his sides and asked for a trot. He picked up a steady pace, concentrating on nothing but Hilary. It felt weird to be riding Satan in a bridle. He didn't need it. After all the training in just a halter, he would turn with a simple shift of his rider's weight. Throughout the ride, he obeyed every one of Hilary's commands and more. He seemed to read her mind. Whatever she was thinking, it seemed as though he was thinking the exact same thing.

For the next couple of days Hilary worked inside the arena. She concentrated on flatwork until she was positive he could handle a trail ride. When Hilary and Amanda rode their horses out in the fields for the first time, Hilary felt a rush of pride tingle up her spine. Here they were, two best friends with two young horses who were quite fond of each other as well.

When they returned from untacking and tending to their horses, they stopped at the side of the grass arena where Elise was having a jumping lesson.

"Her name's Cara," Amanda told Hilary, pointing to the strange instructor inside the ring. "She and Susan are rivals. Ever since they competed against each other in this big show four or five years ago, they've despised one another. See, Susan beat Cara by a sixteenth of a second, and Cara was totally jealous. Now Elise has asked Cara to prep her for the champs, and Susan is pretty mad. I overheard her talking one day, and she said she doesn't want Cara on her property. Especially when Susan could prep Elise the same, if not better," Amanda finished, as the two girls settled themselves on the grass to watch the lesson.

"How annoying to have a complete enemy teach your best student," Hilary said, shaking her head. "Wow, she looks terrific." She watched Elise take a three-foot-six jump like it was nothing.

"Stop that!" Amanda kidded, flicking Hilary in the side. "You'll be just as good in no time at all. Before you know it, you and Satan will be jumping 4'6"!"

"In my dreams," Hilary laughed.

Suddenly looking serious, Amanda shook her head. "No, Hil, I think you could really excel in the East Coast Championships. Take a look around. You've got Susan, the perfect facilities, courage, but most of all, you have Satan. He believes in you, Hil, I know he does."

Hilary thought about this for a minute. Competing in the champs had been a fantasy for the last month—never a goal. *But maybe Amanda's right,* Hilary mused, drifting further into her own thoughts. When she had first come to this farm everyone had doubted her riding ability, particularly Elise. Susan hadn't known she would be such a good stable hand. In addition, the students made fun of her when she joined them in Wednesday lessons. They weren't used to girls older than them being bad riders. They were used to Elise and Amanda, who trained and rode horses exceptionally well. The more Hilary thought about it, though, the harder it was to sort out. How would she learn to jump four feet in only a month's time? And not only that, but how would Satan? He didn't even know how to jump with a rider on his back.

"No, it simply will not work," Hilary told Amanda. "There's just no way."

Amanda didn't look convinced, but she didn't argue.

That night at dinner Hilary told her family all that had gone on in the last few days. Lately she had been so busy at the barn that she'd missed dinner and had to eat on her own. But tonight she had made it to the table and excitedly filled her family in on all that was new in her life. Hilary and Karen decided that it would be best to end her lease on Dolly. She had been a terrific horse for Hilary to learn to ride on, but now that Hilary wouldn't have much time for her, it was unfair to keep the mare. Dolly could teach another child how to ride, and she would get the attention she deserved.

The next morning, Hilary led Satan to the ring. Amanda hadn't shown up, so she'd have to ride without her. Just as Hilary was opening the gate, she noticed Susan on the inside, waiting in the center.

"Ready to work hard?" She asked, smiling.

"Yeah, sure, for what?" Hilary asked.

"For your lesson, silly. You wanted to learn how to jump, today...on Satan."

I did? Hilary was very confused. Seeing the questioning look on her face, Susan said, "You called me last night for a jumping lesson, remember?"

Hilary thought back to the previous evening. As soon as she had gotten home from the barn she and her family sat down to eat. And when Hilary's mom had talked to Susan, it was only about canceling the lease on Dolly. Then it hit her.

"Are you sure it wasn't Amanda calling?" Hilary asked, stroking Satan's black face.

"The caller ID said it was from Amanda's house, but

she said it was Hilary, so I just figured you were spending the night there. Now I see we had a little misunderstanding," she said, shaking her head and laughing.

"Yes, I guess we did. Amanda really wants me to start jumping so..." Hilary said, her voice trailing off.

"So I see nothing wrong in that. Would you like to learn how to jump today?" Susan asked.

"Of course I would, but do you think Satan is ready?"

"Oh, I think he is, Hil. I've watched your progress in the last few days, and you two have made a tremendous leap," Susan said. "Come on, I'll give you a leg up."

Hilary happily agreed and had the most fun she'd ever had on a horse. Satan easily cleared every cross rail Susan set up, and Hilary rode him smoothly. Even Susan was amazed. By the time they'd finished, Hilary was worn out. Satan, however, was still full of energy.

When Hilary finished tending Satan, she jogged over to Amanda's house. She found her lounging beside her pool, soaking up the warm afternoon sun.

"I thought you might find me here," Amanda said.

"Oh please, Manda, on a day like this? Where else would you be?" Hilary joked, taking a seat beside her friend and ripping off her boots.

"So, how was your lesson?" Amanda asked. "You didn't back down, did you?"

"No, I didn't back down—but I could have. What you did was really..." Hilary searched for the right word to say. Perhaps mean or annoying, but instead, Hilary found herself saying, "helpful." Then she smiled and hugged her friend. "Satan was so wonderful, you should have seen him! He jumped everything and so perfectly, too. Susan even said she'd love to ride him, but changed her mind when he tried to nip her."

"Nip her?" Amanda broke in. "As in he bit her?"

"No, but he sort of tried. Why, are you surprised?"

"Well, kind of. It's just that I thought he was totally accustomed to humans now," Amanda admitted.

"No, I'm not sure he'll ever be totally accustomed to us. I saw some kids looking at him in his stall yesterday, and he looked frightened."

"But he's not scared of you, Hil. You're the only person he trusts. That's just so amazing. I wish I had that kind of bond with Silver," Amanda said as Hilary slipped her feet into the soothing pool.

"But you do!" Hilary said. "She loves you."

"Maybe, but Hil, Silver doesn't call to me every time she sees me. Not like Satan."

"No, but Satan also doesn't let innocent children pet him whenever they please," Hilary said.

For the next hour, the two girls shot out compliments to one another. They said so many heartwarming things, that by the time Hilary left, they were both complimented out.

After dinner that evening, Susan called to arrange another lesson. She explained how much talent Hilary and her horse had displayed that day and said they could make it all the way. When Hilary questioned what she meant by "all the way," Susan laughed and said they'd discuss that when the time came.

Hilary thought about what Susan had said as she lay in bed that night. Did she mean Hilary and Satan could make it to the Championships? She couldn't have. Even though Hilary had dreamt of it quite often, she knew she'd never be able to go. Satan probably wouldn't even load into the trailer. And he had never been to a horse show before. He'd go mad!

With that boggling thought, Hilary fell into a restless sleep.

Chapter Nineteen

*H*ilary and Amanda went on a long fitness trot to strengthen the respiration of their mounts. When they returned, both riders and Silver were tired, but Satan was still going strong. When put in his stall, he gazed out of the Dutch doors. Hilary followed his gaze and saw Elise and Cara in the jumping field.

"They're jumping again?" she asked, causing Amanda to pause from her grooming. "I might be wrong, but a book I read the other day said that you should never have a jumping lesson two days in a row."

"Your book was right, Hil, but come on now; that's Elise we're talking about. She rides Lady into the ground," Amanda said, shaking her head.

"Yeah, but doesn't Cara have enough sense to stop her? I mean what ever happened to flatwork?"

"I think they both just really want to win the champs," Amanda answered, continuing her brushing. "See, I kind of think that Cara is reliving her dreams of winning the finals through Elise. She probably thinks that if Elise wins, it will make up for her loss to Susan."

Hilary nodded, bolted Satan's door, and headed out to watch the lesson.

"What brings you here, Hilary; tired of mucking manure?" Elise smirked. She smoothly took a jump then another in a configuration known as an in-and-out. Hilary ignored her comment and took in the scene before her.

Lady was covered in foamy sweat and made a soft grunt over the jumps. Cara kept instructing Elise to keep jumping until the horse remained silent. It was hot that day, and riding in the middle of it made it even worse.

"I will never let you ride in the Championships with your horse sounding like this! Get her together, Elise!" Cara called as she raised the jumps. Hilary saw Elise spur Lady hard. She looked away, unable to watch such cruelty.

Later that afternoon, Hilary headed into the lounge as a reward for completing her chores. As she grabbed a soda from the refrigerator, she saw an envelope with her name on it taped to the handle. She ripped it open and found a note inside:

Hilary,
Meet me at the brook on the Woodland trail at four-thirty. You can take Dolly, and don't tell my mom cause I'm still not supposed to ride.

Jer

As she headed for the trail she noticed Splash was already gone. Come to think of it he had been gone all day. Was Jeremy okay? Thinking of him wounded out in the woods made Hilary shudder. She put that thought out of her head and concentrated on Dolly. Hilary hadn't ridden her since Jeremy's accident. She was happy to feel the familiar horse between her legs. It reminded her that she hadn't spent any time with Jeremy since the accident, either. She kind of missed their time together and wondered if Jeremy did as well. He was kind to Hilary when Elise and his friends weren't around. She came to the conclusion that Jeremy acted the way he did because of peer pressure.

When Hilary reached the brook, she saw Splash tied to a nearby tree. This was the same stream Hilary had visited when she'd seen Elise with Jeremy. After tethering Dolly, Hilary scrambled through the brush and saw him sitting on a rock by the water. She was amazed that he had ridden all this way with the cast on his leg. Luckily for the boy, it didn't cover his knee, so he could still bend it. But it must have been very uncomfortable.

"Hey," Hilary said hesitantly, sitting beside him.

"Hey, what's up? I was worried you wouldn't show," he said in a voice with forced cheerfulness.

"Is everything okay?"

"Yeah, why wouldn't it be?" he asked, scratching his skin under the cast. "Well, actually, this isn't okay. It's been driving me crazy. The doctor said I'm not supposed to ride, but I needed to do some thinking. I come here a lot to think."

"Yeah, you've been out here all day, so I know there's something bothering you."

"Yeah, I do have a reason. It's just—Okay, I feel like

an idiot saying this, but I've been thinking a lot about you lately," Jeremy admitted, looking at the ground.

Hilary gulped, unable to swallow past the lump in her throat. *Did Jeremy just admit to liking me? Is that what he means?*

Glancing up at Hilary's startled face, Jeremy blushed. "You and Satan, I mean," he added quickly. "I'll let you know I'm really jealous. My mom talks about you and that horse every night and how much you've improved. And I just keep thinking that he could have been mine, if only I'd worked harder for him and…"

"Satan is still yours! I'm just kind of riding him for you. I mean, I can help you with him once your leg heals," Hilary interrupted.

"No! You just don't get it, do you? He doesn't want me; he wants you. Look around you, Hil. You're the only one who can touch him. It's not like I can have him trust me the way he does you. Even with your help, he'll never like me." Taking a deep breath, he lowered his voice. "He has a lot of bottled-up talent, Hil. And I'm never going to get anywhere in taking off the lid because we'll never be a team. But you know what? I'm not going to sit around and mope over it. And I'm not going to watch him waste away." Hilary wondered where he was going with this. "Hilary, take him to the Championships for me. Just do it. I know you'll win. Just have faith in him," he urged her, somewhat hysterically.

Hilary thought about what he'd said. Satan was a very good jumper, but from Hilary's point of view they both had a lot to learn first. People would make fun of them. They would be the odd pair out compared to the fancy show horses like Lady.

When Hilary didn't say anything, Jeremy spoke again. "Hil, you're a better rider than you think. You've worked hard, taken lessons, and improved a ton for someone who didn't know a lick about horses. You've got to go for it. What've you got to lose?"

Again Hilary didn't respond. Her hair slipped into her eyes, but she didn't push it away like usual.

"I told my mom this last night," Jeremy said.

"What did she say?" Hilary asked.

"She told me you would have to work really hard. She said she could sign you up for some jumper clinics and things, and you could continue with your lessons. She said if you worked your butt off, you really could do well in the competition."

"You're kidding me! She didn't say that. Did she?" Hilary asked.

"I know you find this hard to believe, but for once I'm not joking," he said. "She told me I would have to help you out, you know, show strategies and things. I could be your groom, Hil; we can be in this together. It'll be great!"

Hilary felt like jumping for joy. Jeremy had worked this all out for her, and although it would be a lot of work, she began to believe she could handle it. She started laughing, half crying as well, and all of a sudden, Jeremy took her in his arms. "You can do it, Hil!" he encouraged, holding her tightly. Hilary smiled contentedly as they leaned back from their embrace. Then Jeremy leaned in and kissed her right on the lips.

That evening Hilary sat with her family at dinner, which didn't happen often anymore. With James' work, Sam's sports, and Hilary's riding, it was difficult to find time.

"Guess what, Mom, Dad," Hilary said, looking from one to the other. "Well, Satan's been going very well for me." She paused and viewed her parents' faces. "See, we've gotten pretty good over the past few weeks, and Susan thinks I could go to the Championships."

"We know, honey," Karen said, "and we're very proud of you. Susan called last night."

"Just think, when we moved here, you barely knew what horses were, and now look at you. You're ready for competition," James added proudly.

Karen nodded. "Hil, we are so happy you've finally found something you enjoy. We're ready to support you in every way possible."

"Even if that means going to the Championships?" Hilary questioned excitedly.

"Even if that means going to the Championships," James repeated.

Across the table Sam rolled his eyes in disgust. "All right, all right already, enough with the cheesiness, please."

Everybody laughed.

"Oh, thank you so much! I love you two," Hilary

squealed, hugging and kissing her parents. "And I love you, too, Sammy," she added, ruffling his hair.

Karen laughed, "Okay, honey. You get up to bed now; I scheduled another jumping lesson for you with Susan tomorrow."

My parents are so wonderful! Hilary thought, strolling up to her room. *They're willing to pay all the expenses Satan and I need to succeed.* Everything was fitting together so perfectly, she wondered if she were dreaming.

Hilary's lesson went well the next day. Susan set up a small course with jumps not exceeding 2'6". She watched as Hilary rode Satan through it with class.

Through every turn Satan remained balanced and attentive to Hilary's commands. She, too, focused on each turn rather than worrying about what lay ahead.

After her lesson, Hilary helped Amanda work with Silver in the ring. Amanda cheered when she heard that Hilary was entered in the Championships. She promised to help her prepare in every way possible.

"So when are you going to the tack store, Hil? You know you're going to need some hefty jumping boots and maybe a breastplate for Satan."

"My mom said she'd take me tomorrow, but I need to go with Susan. She knows the things I need, and my mom has no clue. I would go ask Susan if she could come with us, but right now she's teaching a lesson."

"Yeah, you can ask her later. I want to come, too. I have

to get some supplements for Silver. You don't mind, do you?" Amanda asked as she rode a twenty-meter circle.

"Of course not!"

That evening, Hilary turned Satan out in his private field bordering the edge of the forest far behind the other barns. Satan galloped away into the open space but turned back to Hilary. He ambled over to the fence where she stood watching and quietly rubbed his head on her leg. Then, for some reason, he butted Hilary and threw his head into the air. *He wants to play!* For almost an hour, she frolicked around the new pasture with Satan. They played their silly tag game just like they used to when he was still in the paddock. Finally she kissed him good-night and headed home. She had a lot to prepare.

Chapter Twenty

For the next couple of weeks, Hilary practiced for the looming Championships. Susan gave her a lesson every day except for Saturday and Sunday, when Hilary took a trail ride with Amanda and Jeremy.

The trio had become quite good friends on their long rides together. Hilary and Jeremy kept the kiss from their meeting at the stream a complete secret, but Jeremy's sudden breakup with Elise was quickly known by everyone at Millbrooke.

It was amazing how fast word spread through the stables. A few days earlier, Hilary was a complete "nobody," and now she was a superstar. One of the students must have heard that Hilary was training for the big competition because all the riders knew.

The students who once made fun of Hilary's brown paddock boots and ability to muck out stalls now worshipped her like they did Elise. They followed her around and watched her ride. Even after Hilary's lessons, kids wanted to help her brush Satan, but that, of course, was never going to happen. And instead of the students losing interest when they couldn't get near Satan, they looked up to him and Hilary even more, boosting her self-esteem.

When Hilary, Susan, and Amanda went to the Lewisburg Saddlery that week, she purchased her first pair of shiny, black, tall boots, new show breeches, a set of jumping boots for Satan, and a tasteful leather breastplate. She also bought a hot red saddle pad which stood out brilliantly on Satan's black coat.

There were only three weeks before the big event, and every morning, Hilary got up early and dressed in her riding clothes. Today she had her debut off the property in a jumping clinic with Ralph Bringer. He was a big name in the show-jumping world, and Hilary was thrilled.

Unfortunately, Elise and Lady were going as well, so Susan was trailering both girls' horses—together. Thankfully, it was only an hour's drive.

Hilary ran over to the barn as soon as she was dressed and fetched Satan from his field. She focused her attention on giving him a heavy grooming until he glistened.

When Hilary led him to the trailer, Lady was already loaded. Satan stepped into his slot without a fuss. Before they loaded him, they'd slathered his nostrils with vaseline to keep him from smelling the mare. Her scent could stir up instincts that make a stallion very hard to control.

"So, are you girls excited?" Susan asked, backing out of the drive.

Elise answered first, "Oh please, Susan, I've been to a million clinics, and this one is no different."

"I'm very excited. I still can't believe Satan got in the trailer so well!" Hilary exclaimed.

"I know. He was wonderful for you," replied Susan. "By the way, are your parents coming to watch?"

"My mom is, but dad is stuck at work," answered Hilary. "I gave Mom the directions you gave me last night."

"Great. Now remember, today we aren't expecting much out of him because this is his first time off the farm. We just want him to get some practice jumping strange fences and being with other horses. Don't forget to tell Ralph that."

"Personally, I don't think you should even be going to this, Hilary. Your horse is clearly not ready," Elise muttered so Susan couldn't hear her.

It was obvious Elise was green with envy. She had seemed jealous of Hilary over the last week or so. Not only had Jeremy dumped her for Hilary, but everyone at the barn had, too.

"So, Elise," Susan started, "how are your lessons with Cara going?"

"Wonderfully, thank you. We've been working on Lady's lead swaps after fences. She is doing it perfectly."

"Terrific, I'm happy to hear that," Susan said.

Hilary didn't know how Susan could be so pleasant when Elise was so rude—especially when Susan's show rival was training her best student at her farm. It reminded Hilary of the way Amanda acted toward Elise. Maybe that was how you had to deal with Elise—just turn the other cheek.

Thinking back, Hilary wondered if there was a reason Susan was training her. Did it have something to do with Cara? Was Susan helping Hilary because Cara was helping Elise? Then, at the show, if Hilary won, it would be like Susan winning over Cara. Hilary pushed that thought out of her head. *Susan is helping me because she is a very nice woman,* she assured herself.

When Susan's van pulled into the big parking lot at Ralph Bringer's farm, they hopped out and unloaded the horses. Satan was quivering when he backed out of the trailer. He called out to the other horses on the farm. As he danced in place, Hilary managed to tack him up. Elise did the same for her horse, and soon both girls were ready to mount.

"Why don't we go down to the indoor first?" Susan suggested, walking past a large barn.

The girls examined the fine architecture of the stables as they followed her. The indoor arena had glass windows on all the long sides of the walls, and mirrors covered the short sides. There were already three horses in the ring, and a small crowd sat in the wooden bleachers.

"Hi, Mom!" Hilary said as she led Satan in a small circle. She could tell that her mount was beginning to get a little antsy—and so was she. She wanted to make her mom proud and show her what a wonderful horse Satan was. Karen was a little skeptical of Satan after what had happened to Jeremy.

"Okay, why don't we all mount our horses and begin walking a twenty-meter circle around me," said Ralph, a tall, slender man, slightly bow-legged from all his years of riding.

Satan seemed nervous at Hilary's touch but followed her quiet hand and seat aids. After a few minutes, Ralph asked about each horse and what kind of schooling they had been doing. Then the group picked up a working trot as Ralph explained the importance of a steady rhythm and how it affects jumping. He helped each rider with what they were doing. Then he began an exercise at the canter.

Satan did well in the forty-meter canter circle, halting on four imaginary points, called tangent points. Hilary was elated at how well he responded. Maybe they could succeed at the Championships, she thought.

"This," said Ralph, "will help establish your horse's awareness to your aids, which is very important while jumping. If you don't have the basics for control, there is no way you can successfully jump a course."

He set up a ground pole in the middle of the ring and had everyone canter over it.

"Pretty easy, huh? Now I want all of you to canter over this pole and turn right. The next time you come, turn left," Ralph directed.

The group of riders did as they were told. When they finished, the clinician instructed them to come at the pole on an angle. "This will help you save time in a course of jumps. Taking a jump straight on wastes a lot of time, because once you land, it's hard to turn in time for the next fence, especially if the course is tight. Coming in on an angle helps set you up for the direction you are headed,"

Next, the riders were asked to ride over a cross rail on an angle, then a vertical, and finally an oxer. The vertical was just a simple straight bar while the oxer was a trickier and wider jump. Satan took it beautifully.

"Good boy!" Hilary praised.

Finally, Ralph left the oxer in the middle of the ring and placed a run of cones after the jump, making a path for the riders.

First, they were told to ride it straight on, and when they landed, to turn before the line of cones.

A tall girl on a palomino rode first and had a difficult time turning after the jump. Her horse hit a few of the cones before she successfully made the bend. Then Elise went, and although her turn wasn't the prettiest, she didn't hit any cones. After two more riders had their turns, Hilary rode the obstacle. Satan, being an agile horse, was able to manipulate the bending line without hitting any cones. Then every horse and rider pair rode the layout on an angle, easily avoiding the cones and making the turn.

"I hope I just proved to all of you how important it is to know how to ride a fence on an angle," Ralph said. He explained a few more exercises they could work on at home and ended his clinic.

Hilary hopped off Satan and led him to where her mother waited.

"Hilary, you did wonderfully!" Karen said. She opened her arms to hug Hilary, but the sudden jerk of Satan's head changed her mind. "So...I guess I will see you later tonight." She eyed Satan nervously and walked to her car.

"That was a great workout, wasn't it, girls?" Susan asked as they turned onto the highway and headed home. Hilary agreed and told Susan how proud she was of Satan.

"He trusts you. Nothing will get in his way of pleasing you."

When they got back to Millbrooke, Hilary took Satan to his barn and gave him a long brushing. She removed all the dust from his coat before feeding him a rich meal of bran and molasses. Because of Satan's usual abundance of energy, Hilary released him into his pasture and watched as he collapsed onto the ground and rolled around in the dirt, twisting and turning to make sure every inch of him was dirty. When he stood, he looked back at Hilary and snorted, as though laughing at her. So much for his evening's brushing!

The next morning, as planned on the phone the previous night, Hilary, Amanda, and Jeremy went out for a trail ride. They were just heading across the field toward the woods when they heard a horse cantering up behind them. In unison, they looked to see who was following them. *Great! Elise.*

"How rude of you people not to have invited me!" She scowled, looking from rider to rider. "So I'm coming along anyway." The trio ignored her and continued with their conversation about Satan.

"He was so well behaved, you'd have thought he'd gone to a million clinics," Hilary boasted, patting him on the neck.

"Who knows, Hil? Maybe he has. If he jumped the fence once he can jump it again. For all we know, he could've gone to a midnight clinic and jumped back in his paddock by morning," Jeremy joked, and the girls, with the exception of Elise, laughed.

"Honestly, you three. You're all so immature," she huffed, rolling her eyes. "And Hilary, your dumb pony wasn't that good. You seem to think he's a superstar."

"He is, Elise. No need to be jealous," Amanda said.

"No, he's not. You know why?" Elise seethed. When no one answered her, she continued defiantly. "It's because Lady is a forty-thousand dollar horse, and she has top breeding. She's an Irish sport horse, imported from Ireland, and I'm sorry, Hil, but all you have is a mustang. Everyone knows my horse can out run, out jump, and out fight that…thing," she stammered, pointing to Satan. "I'll show you, Hilary. We'll whip your butt at the Championships, and no one will tell me otherwise."

"I will," Jeremy and Amanda said together.

"Be quiet, you two. I'm talking to Hilary, not you," Elise growled. "I am warning you, Hilary Thompson; back off. You're trying to take my place at Millbrooke; I know it. Susan now favors you, the kids favor you, and worst of all, Jeremy favors you. So step down!" She kicked Lady into a trot and flounced away.

"You okay, Hil?" asked Amanda.

Hilary stared at the pommel of her saddle until she thought she could meet her friends' eyes without frowning. It didn't work.

"Oh, Hil, it's okay. You did nothing wrong; she's just jealous," Amanda soothed, bringing Silver next to Satan and patting her friend on the back.

"Yeah, Amanda's right. Elise's just trying to scare you into not competing," Jeremy added.

"I know, but, maybe she's right. Maybe I should back down. After all, I don't even know what championships are like," Hilary said quietly.

"Hil, no! Don't say that!" Jeremy spluttered. "Elise has never been to the Junior Jumping Champs, either."

"But she's been to all the top shows."

"Come on, Hil. Don't you know who Seabiscuit was?" Amanda urged as they crossed a small stream.

"I saw the movie," Hilary told Amanda.

"Good, and what did everyone think of Seabiscuit in the beginning?"

"Oh, all right, I see where this is going, okay?"

"So? What's the problem? Seabiscuit didn't have good training until later in his life, and no one believed in him, but he still became a champion. Although you might not have had much training, we believe in you, Hil, so you're already better off than that old racehorse!" Amanda finished with a persuasive smile.

"Yeah, Hil, Amanda's right," Jeremy said, winking at Amanda.

"Oh, you guys!" Hilary laughed. She wiped the frown away and grinned at her friends. She could feel her face glowing in the morning sun. She touched the loose strands of damp hair that curled around her velvet cap. She felt very pretty when she laughed at Jeremy's jokes, well aware of her straight, white teeth. She was perfectly relaxed on Satan's back. What would she do without Amanda and Jeremy?

Jeremy rode, laughing at his own lame jokes, with one leg stuck out to the side awkwardly. But he looked very handsome. His brown hair was moist from the sweat trickling down his face, and now, riding shirtless—after insisting it had grown much too hot—he showed off his trim physique.

Two weeks passed like the puffs of a dandelion blown into the wind. Hilary kept a careful watch on Satan, riding him in the early mornings to avoid the heat. She observed the condition of his legs and the width of his barrel, making sure he didn't get overweight. She added an extra dose of electrolytes to his feed because he'd been sweating regularly during his intense workouts.

Hilary's riding had improved since her clinic with Ralph, and so had Satan's jumping. With every fence they took, he would snap up his knees and hold them tightly to his chest until they'd safely cleared the jump. Everything seemed on track for their departure to the Championships. Hilary could hardly wait.

She and Susan were leaving for the Championships the next day. The first day was for horse and riders to settle in. The competition officially started on Friday, when the first round of the event was to kick off. Only fifteen horses could move on to the next level. Round two would be held on Saturday, when the qualifying rounds for the jump-off were held. Finally on Sunday, the finalists would compete for the blue ribbon.

Because Elise was traveling with Cara, there would be plenty of room in the van for Silver, who would be Satan's pal for the weekend. Amanda and Jeremy were going along to give Hilary mental and physical support. Karen, James, and Sam would arrive as the cheering squad for Hilary.

"Good night, boy. I'll see you bright and early, okay?" Hilary told Satan after a long chat under the stars.

It seemed like only yesterday that she had snuck in her midnight rides on this horse. Now look at the two of them—off to the Championships in Lexington, Kentucky. Although they had only the slightest chance of winning, Hilary felt like a champion already.

Chapter Twenty-one

"Beep, beep, beep, beep," screeched Hilary's alarm clock at 4:45 in the morning. It was time. It was Thursday, the big day. The very big day.

"Rise and shine, my dear," Karen said, opening Hilary's door. "I'll make you a big breakfast while you get dressed, okay?"

"Sounds good, just don't make too much food, I'm kind of…"

"Nervous," Karen supplied. "It's only natural at a time like this, honey."

When Hilary lugged her suitcase into the kitchen, Karen, James, and Sam were waiting. Because of work and Sam's scheduled activities, Hilary's family wouldn't be arriving at the show until Friday.

When she finished her breakfast, James drove her to Millbrooke and loaded her suitcase into Susan's van.

"Okay then, it looks like we're all set," Susan said. "We have our luggage; we have food and water for us and the horses, hay nets, and bedding in the trailer. And I packed grain for Satan and Silver for the weekend."

"Great, thank you, Susan." Hilary said, doing her own

mental check to make sure everything she needed was in the van.

She had her clothes—riding and casual— her tack and grooming supplies, and all Satan's health records. All she needed was her horse.

"All right, you get Satan and I'll get Silver because I don't know where Amanda is—oh there she is—good morning, Amanda!" Susan called, as the blonde-haired girl ran toward them from the parking lot.

"'Morning. Sorry I'm late, Susan. My alarm clock never went off," she said. Turning to Hilary, she asked, "Nervous?"

"Very."

"Okay girls, we can have small talk later, but let's load these horses first," Susan said, handing Amanda Silver's lead rope.

Once the horses were safely in the trailer, they did one last check to make sure they had everything. The horses had wraps on their legs to protect them during the ride, and they munched tranquilly on their hay.

"Okay everybody, hop in the van. We're just waiting on Jeremy now," Susan announced as she situated herself in the driver's seat.

"Where is he?" Hilary asked, taking shotgun.

"You'll see," Susan answered.

A few minutes later, Jeremy came hopping down from the house with a huge present in his arms. It was difficult to hold while on crutches. Hilary got out of the van to meet him.

"Here, you'll like it," he said, handing her the big gift in shiny blue wrapping paper. "Mom helped me make it. Well, actually she did a lot since I can't sew," he admitted, laughing. "But it was my idea."

Hilary tore off the paper and saw a folded cotton blanket. It was bright red, just like Satan's saddle pad, and extremely soft.

"Thank you so much. It's beautiful, Jer," she said, stepping forward to hug him. Jeremy pushed her back.

"You didn't even open it. Unfold it," he instructed.

Hilary did and gasped at what she saw. She had thought it was an extra large blanket, but it was a cooler for Satan. It had rich black letters on each side reading,

~ Satan ~

The belly, chest and leg straps were also black with gold glitter shimmering in the light of the rising sun.

Now Jeremy accepted Hilary's gratitude.

"Alrighty everybody, it's straight forward from here," said Susan, making the first turn onto the highway.

"How long is it going to take us?" asked Amanda from the backseat with Jeremy.

"Somewhere between three and four hours, I'd say. Not too bad, really. Remember kids, this is for the entire east coast, so some people are coming all the way from Maine and even Florida."

Before long, the passing cars became a blur, and Amanda, Jeremy, and Hilary fell fast asleep. Soon Susan aroused them from their rest. "We're almost there," she said.

One by one, they lifted their heads to ask what time it was and how long they'd been asleep.

"You've been asleep since we reached the turnpike. I didn't think you guys would sleep that long." She laughed, watching the six groggy eyes take in the scenery. "And it's only ten thirty. We're supposed to check-in by eleven, so we're right on time."

As Hilary looked out the window, a very large farm caught her eye. It was loaded with trailers, horses, and people. There were arenas everywhere—indoor and out.

Susan put on her blinker and said, "We're here!"

Hilary gasped, "I never imagined it was this large!"

"Me neither," said Amanda. Jeremy simply stared out the window with his mouth hanging open.

The van turned into the driveway and passed a large sign that had a picture of a mare and foal. It read:

KENTUCKY NATIONAL HORSE PARK

Tied on the bright white fencing, one on either side of the drive, two banners read:

EAST COAST JUNIOR JUMPER FINALS

Everyone broke into excited chatter, but soon quieted as the rig in front of Susan's pulled away and continued into the park.

"Good mornin', ma'am; fine day, isn't it?" asked a fleshy man at a booth where all the trailers were stopping. "Can I have your competitor's first and last name, please?"

"Certainly, it's Hilary Thompson, and she is riding Satan," Susan said. He checked something off on his list.

"He must be a real devil," the man chuckled to himself. "Can I see his Coggins test please?"

As Susan looked through her paperwork, Hilary thought back to how difficult it had been for the vet to draw blood for the Coggins test earlier that week. Satan hadn't wanted to hold still and wouldn't let the veterinarian touch him without Hilary by his head.

"Okay, ma'm, you're all set. You're located in barn number five, and here's a packet for you," he said, handing Susan a manila envelope. "It has all the information on your ride times, our sponsors, and fun activities for the weekend."

"Thank you so much, sir." Susan smiled.

"You're welcome. Have a good day and good luck in the finals," he said. Hilary gulped. Looking around at all the fancy horses, she knew she'd need it.

Susan drove to barn five, and everyone jumped out, happy to stretch their legs. With all four of them working, it only took a few minutes to bed both horses' stalls and clip up their buckets. They put a few flakes of hay in the stalls. Now they were ready to unload Silver and Satan and introduce them to their beds.

"Okay, now back him out slowly," Susan called to Hilary as Satan stepped down the ramp.

The trailer was hot, and both horses had worked up quite a sweat. Satan, shaking with excitement, pulled at the lead as he stepped onto the ground.

"Easy, boy, easy," Hilary soothed, stroking his neck.

But it wasn't working. Looking around got Satan even more worked up. As Silver kicked inside the trailer, eager for her turn to get out, he sidestepped and whinnied frantically.

Amanda hurried to untie Silver. Susan unlocked the bar behind the mare's rump, which sent her catapulting down the ramp. Amanda lost her grip and fell to the floor when Silver pulled away, but Susan grabbed the mare's lead before she could escape. When Satan reared up in alarm, Hilary eased him back down.

"Steady now!" Susan said, pulling on Silver's lead. "Get him to his stall," she called to Hilary, who was being dragged in circles by Satan.

Susan put Silver in her stall and ran back to help Hilary. She reached for the lead rope so quickly, it spooked Satan. He pulled back, yanking the lead rope from Susan's hand. He tore off, stampeding through the barns.

"Loose horse!" people called, jumping out of his way.

"Everyone grab a lead rope; we've got to catch him," Susan hollered as Amanda, Jeremy, and Hilary followed her through the barns.

Satan galloped through the barns, the parking lot, and a few neighboring fields. Other horses at the park became riled up, and some broke away from their handlers. A voice on an intercom asked everyone to take part in catching the horses. All the people running around may have deterred some of the loose horses, but it only panicked Satan more.

After fifteen minutes of constant running, Hilary caught up to her horse, who stood in the middle of a parking lot, dazed. When she grabbed his lead rope he once again stood up on two legs, causing the spectators to "ooooh" and "aaaah." When his legs reached the ground once more, Hilary led him back to barn five as he jigged nervously beside her.

After soothing her horse and rubbing a cooling liniment on his legs, Hilary and her helpers piled into the truck and drove to their hotel. It was a small resort a mile from the park. It was filled with other competitors.

Everyone unpacked and settled into their room before heading back to the barns to check on the horses. Once all was okay, Hilary, Susan, Amanda, and Jeremy attended the opening ceremony for the finals in the huge coliseum.

The ceremony included a parade of trotters, mini ponies, carriage horses, dressage horses, and Clydesdales. Last year's junior finalist gave a good-luck prep speech to all the competitors. The man who had designed the jumping courses for the next few days explained what kinds of challenges to expect from them.

When it was all over, Susan took everybody out for a big dinner since they had missed lunch. They returned to the hotel around seven.

"I suggest everyone get to sleep early. It's going to be a very big day tomorrow," Susan said. "Hilary, you come with me. We're going to go through the packet, so you can learn the schedule for your rides, and rehearse your jump strategies."

Hilary followed her to the hotel lobby, and they sat on a leather couch. In front of them, a fake fire blazed. It distracted Hilary for a moment because it was late summer—not winter.

"Hil, I'm sorry about earlier. I know it was my fault your horse broke away," Susan said.

"No, it wasn't your fault. He was nervous," Hilary said, even though she knew Susan was right.

"Well, all right, let's get down to business. Tomorrow you only ride once. It's called Round One of the competition," she said, tapping her pen on the packet. "It says here that, based on your score, you will either advance to Round Two, or you will not. You have to go clear and have very few, if any, time faults, if you want to continue. Remember—these are the Championships." Hilary nodded, taking in every word Susan said.

"On Saturday you will ride Round Two, assuming you make it. It says we will get a phone call Friday evening from one of the officials to tell us if you moved on to the next round," she explained. "Round One basically eliminates the horses that really shouldn't be here. Normally that consists of the horses that didn't go to the qualifiers, which includes you. But you will do fine; Satan is different than some of those other horses. Round Two is where you want to do your best. If you get past this, you move to the final round, Round Three: the jump-off. If you win Round Three, you win the competition. You with me?"

"Yeah, I'm with you, but there's probably no point in explaining Round Two to me," Hilary said.

"Hilary, if you're going to think in that negative manner, there really is no point, is there?" Susan said sharply. "You have to believe in yourself, but most of all, you must have faith in Satan. If he's the horse I remember, he will give it his all. You just have to help him through it."

"You're exactly right. I'm sorry," Hilary apologized.

For the next half hour, Susan described every possible scenario that could go wrong while jumping and told Hilary how to fix it. She went into depth on how to ride tight turns, straight lines, and to know how fast to push Satan.

When she finally finished, Hilary's brain felt like it was drowning in a sea of information. Yet she felt more ready than she had before. Hilary thanked Susan for her prep talk, and they headed back to their room to get some rest.

Chapter Twenty-two

"Up and at 'em!" Susan said cheerfully the next morning. "We have a very busy day ahead of us."

Amanda and Hilary staggered out of bed and went into the bathroom to get dressed. Jeremy, who wasn't much of an early bird, didn't even budge until his mom placed a wet cloth on his head.

"Okay, okay, I'll get up," he said, still not moving.

"Jeremy, let's go," Susan said seriously, as he grudgingly rolled out of bed.

Once the crew was dressed and fed, they jumped in the truck and headed for the park. They fed the horses their breakfast and mucked out the stalls. Hilary and Amanda walked Satan and Silver around the show ground for a good hour, to stretch out their muscles and keep their joints from swelling. This allowed Satan to get used to the surroundings as Hilary scoped out the arenas and the jumps. At eight, the rides had just started, so they stopped to watch a few of them. The footing in the rings was great, but the jumps looked exceedingly high. Today they were supposed to be between 3'3" and 3'6", but to Hilary they looked humongous. She couldn't imagine how tall they'd be in Round Three.

"Come on, Hil," Amanda said, "let's take these guys back now."

"Okay, but I think I'll come back later with Susan, so she and I can go over the course."

"Sounds good. Maybe I'll come, too."

The girls led the horses back and put them in their stalls. They couldn't find Susan or Jeremy. *Maybe they went to look at the ride times*, thought Hilary.

"It says you ride at 3:46 in ring four," said Amanda, reading from the packet they'd been given when they checked in. "I saw that ring. I think they have four rings running for the day."

"Yeah, I think so, too. Gosh there must be a lot of competitors," Hilary muttered. "Let's go look at ring four again, just to make sure we know where it is."

"Now we have rider number one hundred four, Elise Cabarete on Lady Marmalade," said the announcer.

"Do you think she'll go clean?" asked Amanda, biting her lips nervously.

"I'll give you one guess," Jeremy's voice said.

"Where've you been, Jer?" asked Hilary, scooting over to make room for him on the bleachers.

"Mom and I went to say hi to some of her old friends," he said. "She makes her rounds at all the big shows and loves to drag me with her. We came to watch Elise ride."

The girls nodded in response, but their eyes were fixed on the horse and rider before them.

Lady cleared the first jump with ease and went on to tackle the next combination. The rest of the jumps were very smooth. Elise had gone clean with an exceptional time of 75.3 seconds. This put her in second place so far.

The next few riders were mixed. Some had time penalties while others knocked down rails. Those who hadn't attended the qualifiers made it visible in their rounds as very few moved to the second. Even so, Hilary got a good idea of how to ride the course by watching so many horses in the ring. She knew the order of the jumps and rehearsed it in her head to make sure she had it down pat.

Susan came over and told her to go get Satan ready for his own ride. "You'll want plenty of time to warm up because we don't know how full of himself he'll be." Susan explained as they walked back to the barns. "Now I want you to warm up just like we do for a jumping lesson at home, okay? Start with a long walk, especially since he was in all night. Then pick up a trot and let him go around on a nice, loose rein. Work him in both directions and make twenty-meter circles. Make sure he bends his body. Then you can canter in both directions and do circles. Once you've done all that, I'll give you some jumps to tackle."

When Satan was completely groomed and tacked up, he looked like a star. He wore brown jumping boots on all four legs and red bell boots on his front hooves. His red saddle pad matched his other gear, and his saddle gleamed. He wore his leather breastplate to keep the saddle from slipping back. His bridle was clean and sparkling, and he wore a mild snaffle bit. Hilary didn't understand why so many of the riders here had big bits for their horses. From her point of view a rider should know how to steer and control the horse through his legs and seat. She supposed that was easy for her to say, for she had ridden Satan without a bridle for at least three weeks while she was training him.

Hilary looked presentable, too. With her black tall boots and white riding breeches, she looked just like all the other riders, if not better. Her black coat molded to her thin waist and matched her boots and hard hat. Underneath the coat she wore a crisp white show shirt. Susan insisted that Hilary take a crop, just in case she needed to wake Satan up. Hilary insisted right back that she would never use it on him, but agreed to carry it along with her anyway. Amanda and Jeremy followed Susan and Hilary to the ring to watch her warm up. The ring was very crowded but soon cleared out as riders left to compete in their rounds.

"Put him through his paces," Susan said as she joined her son on the bench. "I'll come in when it's time to jump."

Hilary did her best to warm Satan up, but he kept spooking at all the activity taking place outside the ring. When people ran by, he shot forward and sometimes leapt into the air. He called out to other horses that were coming and going. When they responded, he pulled at the bit and tossed his head, unable to focus. Finally Susan came in and set up a cross rail for him to jump. He cleared it with miles to spare but threw his head in the air and took off afterwards. Luckily, Hilary was able to slow him down and take him over it again.

"Okay, Hilary, you're in the hole. That means you have two riders still ahead of you. Why don't we head over to the ring?" Susan opened the gate for Satan and walked to ring four.

Hilary felt like jelly. She was so nervous about going into the ring that she barely heard Susan's last prep talk about the course.

"Next up is number two hundred nine, Hilary Thompson riding Satan," the loud speaker rang as Hilary trotted into the ring.

She heard people in the crowd mutter, "Look it's the devil horse," or, "That's the horse that got loose." She ignored them and concentrated on Satan. He emitted a long, nasal snort.

"Come on, boy," urged Hilary, begging for his attention. She cantered him in a complete hunter circle before crossing through the start flags. Although her heart felt like it would beat out of her chest, she focused her whole mind solely on jumping.

Approaching the first fence, Satan was the opposite of focused. He tossed his head in the air and got too close to it. Hilary held her breath as he lurched over the jump, throwing her onto his neck. She scrambled back in the saddle and looked up just in time for a combination with bright colored sailboats, serving as standards holding up the poles. He jumped the first one smoothly but stumbled after the second jump and bucked playfully. Hilary heard the crowd's muffled laughter. She pulled his head up and forced him to pay attention. The next jump was an imposing oxer, at least 3'4", and there was no time for play.

His sudden boost of spirit was his first sign of effort as he soared over the jump easily. Hilary praised him and pushed him on to another combination. He cleared the first jump but sent the next jump's pole rumbling to the ground. After hitting the rail, Satan gave another buck, harder than before. Hilary managed to hold herself in the saddle and hang on as they whipped around a tight turn to a jump with a Liverpool. His jump wasn't pretty, but he managed to go clean. After clearing a Swedish oxer with two sets of slanted rails and twisting around a dangerously tight turn, they came to the last challenge—a triple combination. Hilary held her breath as her horse carried her over the first, the second, the third, and through the finish flags. She stroked Satan's neck as she stopped to hear if she had any time faults.

"And that was Hilary Thompson with four jumping penalties and eight time faults." Her heart dropped.

Hilary's parents ran up to her when she came out of the ring and congratulated her for such a "good round." Susan, Jeremy, and Amanda helped her dismount. Susan didn't say anything, but Hilary knew she was disappointed. Satan pranced the whole way back to barn five. Amanda helped Hilary apply liniment, which acted as a cooling aid, to his legs. When they finished caring for him, they walked to the main office of the show grounds to look at the scoreboards.

"I guess I'm not competing tomorrow," Hilary said, viewing all the clear rounds for that day.

"Don't say that, Hil. There are still plenty of riders to go," Amanda said, although she had to know there was a very small chance that Hilary and Satan would proceed to the next course.

"Oh, we could have done so much better," Hilary said to Satan later that evening. "It's my fault, too, I shouldn't have gotten so nervous." She rubbed his neck as he nuzzled her hair.

It was late, and most of the competitors had gone to their hotels for the night. Hilary had insisted that Susan, Amanda, and Jeremy leave as well, so they could take showers back at the inn. She had told them she needed some time with Satan—alone. He seemed to sense that Hilary wasn't feeling like herself, for when she tried to leave, he nickered and stepped in front of the stall door. The rays of moonlight that seeped into the stall painted him in a warm glow, and Hilary sighed deeply. How she hated to leave him!

"I have to go so I don't miss the phone call that tells us we can no longer compete," she grumbled. "Good night."

Back at the hotel, Hilary quietly lay on her bed staring at the ceiling while everyone else played cards. Her parents and Sam had the hotel room next door but joined the rest to wait for the phone call.

When the phone finally rang, everyone grew silent.

Hilary gulped and picked up the receiver before the first ring had ended.

"Hello?" she said, her voice cracking.

"Hi, is this Hilary Thompson?"

"Yes, this is she."

"I'm from the main office at the park, and I just want to let you know that you've made it to Round Two," said the man's voice. "Hello? Hello?"

Hilary shakily set down the phone. *Was this really happening? How could she have made it to the next round?* Amazed, she lay on the bed next to the phone. She turned over and stuffed her head under the pillow to see if she was dreaming. She knew everyone would figure she was crying, and sure enough, they came over to comfort her. When she pulled her head out from under the pillow, the group looked stunned. She was smiling.

"I made it!" she cried.

Not only had Hilary found the call unbelievable, but no one else could believe it, either. Just to make sure, Susan called the office back and asked them to repeat Hilary's news.

"Okay, thanks so much, sir." Susan hung up the phone. Turning to the others, she said, "He thought the phone must have been cut off, but indeed, he confirmed it." Hilary and Satan would compete in Round Two.

Chapter Twenty-three

*H*ilary lay awake looking at the alarm clock beside her bed. She was exhausted yet unable to get any rest. It was just three in the morning; they wouldn't be leaving for the stables until after six. Hilary groaned. She didn't know if she could wait that long to see Satan, and she didn't know if her stomach could, either. She wanted to tell her horse the great news she had received the night before: they would be riding at 12:15 in Round Two of the Championships.

After thinking through her course strategy over and over, Hilary finally began drifting off to sleep. At the same time, the telephone rang, announcing the arrival of six AM. Forgetting how tired she was, she leapt out of bed and ran to where she had carefully laid out her show clothes the night before. After dressing, she anxiously waited for everyone else to get ready for the day.

"You'll really have to push him around this turn because it's going to waste time," Susan coached as she and Hilary walked the course later that morning. It looked trickier than yesterday's course. The turns were tight, and it was meant to be ridden fast. The jumps ranged between 3'6" and 4'0", but Susan told Hilary to ride every one of them like they were ten feet high.

"You have to be precise. Ride for straightness unless you have a really tight turn like jump number six," Susan said, indicating a combination with a tight turn to a triple. If you have the opportunity, push him a bit and ask for a gallop. We want to save as much time as we can."

After walking the course, Susan left to find out how many riders had made it to the next round. She told Hilary to go get Satan ready. When Hilary reached barn five, she saw an all too familiar figure by her horse's stall.

"Elise, what are you doing?" Hilary asked.

"Oh, Hilary, I just came by to congratulate you on your pathetic round yesterday. You did an awesome job hanging onto Satan's neck," she said sarcastically, smiling in her artificial manner. "Oh, and have you looked at the scores yet? I was the third person proceeding to the next round, and you," she laughed, "you are thirty-third, which was the last rider accepted."

Hilary gulped. That was pretty bad. She wondered if Susan knew that and just hadn't mentioned it to her.

"Let me tell you this, dear, maybe it will make you feel better. Some people only beat you by sixteenths of a second, but every second counts. You know what I mean?" Elise walked away, leaving Hilary annoyed.

"We'll show her, won't we, boy?" she said, cupping her mustang's muzzle in her hand.

By the time she reached the warm-up arena to prepare for her round, Susan was already there, setting up jumps.

"Hilary, there you are! Where have you been?" she asked. "Get in here and start riding."

For whatever reason, Satan warmed up well that day and actually focused on his job. Maybe he sensed Hilary's feeling that they had nothing to lose. After yesterday's round, they could only get better. Hilary went over the course at least three times in her head and five with Susan. By the time she was due in the ring, she was feeling more confident and secure than she had the previous day.

She took a deep breath before riding her beginning circle. She flew through the start flags at an already fast pace. She steadied Satan a few strides away from the first fence and soared over it, clearing the top pole with inches to spare. At the second fence Satan jumped so high she thought he'd never land. Hilary smiled to herself but knew they'd wasted some time. They would have to jump the fences flat, so they were in the air for the shortest amount of time.

She urged him forward as they galloped around a tight turn to the third fence. Here they rode a double oxer and galloped on to an ascending triple bar. With flaming determination they flew over it. Hilary counted strides to the next fence. Satan popped over the fifth jump, shifting Hilary slightly out of the saddle.

She turned her head to look at the sixth. This was the tough one. By now, however, Satan was raring to go, and he didn't listen to Hilary's commands to slow down. Two jumps with yellow standards made the first combination, which they rode too quickly, but at least they were clear. Hilary turned him sharply and took a triple combination. Messy, but clear!

After flying over a green roll top, there were only two jumps left to go. They would have to be ridden carefully. Hilary tightened her grip on the reins and steadied her mount for the next fence. She figured they were fine on time, so they could focus on getting over the jumps cleanly. Hilary set Satan up on an angle, thinking of her clinic with Ralph and how much angling helped make tight turns. The next and final bending line had the sharpest turn in the course. They cleared the first one, but had to immediately hit the brakes when they landed. Satan grunted loudly but managed to whip around the turn and clear the last fence. Hilary squeezed his sides, and they tore off for the finish flags.

"A great round by Hilary Thompson, with no jumping faults and no time faults," the announcer sang.

Hilary, euphoric, rode Satan out of the ring. Despite her constant nagging at him to pay attention, it had ended in a great ride.

"Good boy!" she cheered, dismounting and hugging his lathered neck. She was overcome by hugs and kisses and "great jobs" from all her fans in the crowd. As Hilary led him back to the barn, however, she got the slightest feeling that something was wrong with him.

"Does he seem tired to you guys?" Hilary asked Amanda and Jeremy when they reached the barn.

"Yes, and he should be," Amanda laughed. "He just delivered a great round."

"Not to mention how fast he went," Jeremy said.

"I know but..." Hilary began, thinking this through. "Oh, never mind," she told her friends, but it was still very much on her mind.

As she untacked, she thought of all the long, hard rides she'd had with Satan. Never once had he shown signs of fatigue or even the slightest droop of his spirit. It just wasn't like him. After rubbing his legs with the usual cooling gel and giving him all the love he could handle, she turned out the barn lights and met everyone at the van.

"So...should we go out for another celebratory meal?" Susan questioned, looking at all the faces surrounding her. Sam jumped up and down, and Jeremy joined him jokingly.

"Let's! It will be our treat," Karen announced, hugging Hilary tightly.

Chapter Twenty-four

The fair grounds buzzed with action. Horses and their handlers crowded the walk-ways, and the quiet hum of their hooves on black-top echoed through the vicinity. There was an air about the place; the kind of feeling that precedes a big event. It hovered in the humid air that was trapped inside the Kentucky Horse Park.

The sky was gray, and dark storm clouds lingered far off in the distance. Hilary hoped it wouldn't rain. Everyone was antsy, and there was little cure for their nerves until the day came to an end, nearly ten hours away.

The competitors crowded the show arena for two hours, while everyone got a taste of the final course. Susan and Hilary walked it five times, reviewing how she would ride each fence. When finished, they checked the scores to see who else had made it to the final round.

"Oh, good, Elise made it!" Susan said happily, pointing to her name on the board. *Oh, gee, I'm so happy,* Hilary thought, still amazed at Susan's generosity.

"And look, Hilary! You had the fourth fastest time

yesterday," Susan enthused. "And my, my, my, would you look at that?" Hilary followed her gaze and saw that the fastest time belonged to Elise.

"That girl has really improved. She used to place around fifth at big shows like these, and now look at her time!"

Hilary went back to the barn after "mind riding" the course once more. She tacked up Satan and took him to the ring to warm up. There were horses everywhere, cantering to jumps, trotting circles, and waiting by the ringside with their owners. Riders would holler, "Cross-rail," as they charged through the crowd and leapt over a fence, often colliding with others who had the same intentions.

Looking across the crowds of people, Hilary saw a big hay field and beyond that, trees. *Woods!* She decided no one would mind if she took a warm-up walk through them, so winding through the clumps of spectators watching the warm-up rings, she headed across the fields. She allowed Satan to canter through the field as he pleased. He didn't try to grab at the bit or take off; he just glided across the tall grass like a deer.

As Satan moved gracefully, Hilary's mind wandered back to his days of training. She imagined herself cantering in his corral by moonlight, as she had done so many times before. After her thoughts cleared, she eased him to a gentle walk and turned him around—almost reluctantly. She couldn't wait until the show was over, so she and Satan could gallop through the fields back at home. But today they had a job to do. With Hilary stroking his neck, they exited the field. To her horror, the speakers rang, "And now we have our last rider of the day, Hilary Thompson on Satan."

Hilary froze. How long had she been out there? She was sure it had only been for a short while, although the walk back had taken some time. But even so, she had given herself nearly an hour's warm-up before her class was said to begin. However, seeing the empty warm-up ring, she knew that her mind must have slipped.

"Hilary, where on God's earth have you been? Are you warmed up? I couldn't find you. Just get in there and ride the way we practiced!" Susan hollered, clearly in a state of panic. "You must go fast; the previous riders were booking!"

Satan, now totally content after their walk in the field, responded to Hilary's signals and flew through the start flags. They cleared the first jump at what felt like sixty miles per hour. Yesterday Hilary would have asked him to slow down, but not today. The gallop through the field reminded her of how much Satan trusted her. She had to trust him, as well, by letting him pick the pace.

So far that weekend, they had not worked as a team. Although they had gone clear yesterday, it was obvious that Hilary had made all the decisions. Today, however, they were a team. They were working together as horse and rider should. They soared over the next fence, followed by two triple combinations in a row.

"I love you," Hilary whispered as they rode a bending line like it was nothing.

It seemed to Hilary that she and Satan were the only creatures in the world, jumping the course for pure love of the sport. All too soon, however, the last jump came up and Hilary felt herself being drawn back into reality. Satan gave one last mighty leap and landed safely on the other side. Suddenly he was heaving. With one last effort, Satan and Hilary surged across the finish line like a meteor streaking through the sky.

"And they've won," Hilary heard the announcer say.

"Satan and Hilary have won this year's Junior Jumping Finals with a time of 70.12 seconds!"

The crowd began to cheer, but Hilary barely heard them. The rain had begun to fall from the sky, and drops blurred her vision. She leapt off Satan's back and took off the saddle. Jeremy replaced it with his cooler. She was smothered with hugs and kisses, but she pulled away.

"Something's wrong with Satan, I know it!" she cried, leading him away from the roaring crowd as thunder echoed loudly above them.

"I need a vet! Get a vet, somebody!" she shrieked, as tears began to mix with the rain that streamed down her face.

Satan was now pawing the ground, and his raspy breath was erratic. Blood trickled down his nose. A vet pushed through the crowd ordering everyone to step back. Once safely in the center of the mass, she reached into her vet bag to get something for the sick horse. But it was too late. The black mustang dropped to the ground.

"Satan!" Hilary gasped after the deafening thud. Dropping with him, she slid her arm under his jaw to support his head. "No!"

Satan lifted his head and looked into Hilary's eye one final time. Then his gentle eyes closed. The vet placed her index finger under the horse's jaw and shook her head. Looking around at the crowd, she stood up and said, "He's gone."

Chapter Twenty-five

A week later, Hilary stared out her bedroom window as she had done so many months before. In her hands she clenched Satan's red cooler. The autopsy report from his sudden death had come that day. He had suffered an aortic aneurysm. Now all the memories of last week, which Hilary had tried to push away, came flooding back like a river of sorrow. The veterinarians had assured Hilary and everyone at Millbrooke Stables that nothing could have been done to save him. Hilary was sure it was because he had been overworked, but the vets told her otherwise; it was no one's fault.

"He must have had a weak heart as a foal," they'd said. "It's common in wild horses whose mothers are malnourished when they are born. And whether he had been in his stall, a field, a trailer, or in our case, a horse show, he would have died."

They had buried Satan at the park itself, and a statue was being made in memory of him. With Satan, Hilary had buried the silver trophy he had won for her. She knew it belonged to him more than anyone else. She would always remember that competition in her heart and didn't need a trophy to recall what a wonderful horse he had been.

Smiling sadly, she hugged the cooler close to her chest, clenching the autopsy report in her hands. Soon she would have to tell Susan, her parents, and everyone else from the stables what the report said—just not yet. She didn't want to think back on all the memories she had with that horse; it was too painful.

But as Hilary sat in her bed, staring vacantly out the window as memories of Satan filled her mind. The first day she had seen him and how he had nearly flown across the fields in fear. Her very first time stroking his long, black face, the first time on his back, the first time over a jump. Hilary realized Satan was a horse she would never forget no matter how hard she tried. She couldn't just push those thoughts out of her head as she had tried so hard to do that past week. They just didn't want to leave. Hilary slipped off her bed and spread the cooler over it like a throw rug. She heard a knock on the front door and paused. She didn't feel like talking to anyone. Closing her door, she settled back on her bed and stared out the window.

But it was no use. The visitors found her. "Hilary?" Amanda gently urged as she, Jeremy, and Elise slipped in and settled themselves on the floor next to her bed. "How are you feeling today?"

Amanda and Jeremy had been to Hilary's house every other day since the death of Satan. Hilary appreciated their dedication, especially when they just sat silently, but nothing anyone could do or say could take away her pain.

She had not visited the stables all week. It would be too upsetting for her, and her friends told her they understood that. They just didn't want her alone all day when both her parents and Sam were gone until the evening. Elise, however, had not visited before. She had received third place at the competition and was livid at Hilary for beating her. But before Elise could give her a hard time...well, after what happened, even Elise couldn't be so cruel.

"Hilary," Elise began uncertainly, nibbling on her bottom lip. Hilary wondered if she was trying to apologize for all the mean things she had ever said about Satan, but after a moment she just reached for Hilary's limp hand and clasped it in her own. "You can ride Lady anytime you want." Her voice cracked, and she looked Hilary in the eye, smiling sadly.

A month before, Hilary would've been astonished by the change in Elise's behavior. Today it didn't even make an impact.

"Thanks, Elise," she managed to whisper. Then Jeremy saw the letter still crumpled tightly in Hilary's hand.

"May I?" he asked, as Hilary allowed him to take it from her hand. Elise, Jeremy, and Amanda each read the autopsy report silently before returning it to Hilary.

Exchanging a nervous glance with Jeremy, Amanda said, "Umm, Hil? There's something outside we want to show you."

Without saying anything more, Jeremy took Hilary's hand in his and turned toward the door. Sighing, she stood up and plodded down stairs and out the front door.

She saw Susan holding a little bay horse that much resembled Satan. Smiling warmly, Susan said, "Hilary, we bought him from the mustang adoption agency—the same one Satan came from."

Hilary slowly pushed the fog from her mind to take in the scene before her.

"He's been at the agency for a while, so some of the workers there taught him to lead. He came from a mare from Satan's herd. She foaled soon after she came to the agency," Susan continued. "Hilary, they believe this is Satan's son, and he's all yours."

Hilary began to cry as she went to the little horse. She cried both tears of sadness and tears of joy.

"He's two years old and nameless, so you better come up with something soon," teased Jeremy, who obviously, along with Amanda and Elise, had known all about the little bay.

Hilary spent the rest of the day with her friends, playing with the young gelding and searching for the perfect name. Finally, she found it. She would call him Promise—Satan's Promise. As the little bay horse nuzzled her arm, she understood that he would help her move forward with her life. He would always be a reminder of all the lessons Satan had taught her, and with him, she could pull through. But she would never forget her Satan. He would remain in Hilary's heart as the little black mustang she would remember forever.

Hilary's Glossary of Horse Terms

Arena: Also known as a riding ring; an enclosed space in which to ride.

Appaloosa: A breed of horses that have spots. These horses were first used by the Native Americans.

Bay: A horse with a deep reddish body color and a black mane and tail. There can be different types: a blood bay, which is a brighter red or a seal bay which is darker.

Bell Boots: A bell-shaped covering made of rubber that fastens around the horse's hooves to protect his heels.

Boarders: People who pay to keep their horses at a farm that they do not own.

Breastplate: An article of tack that is used to prevent the saddle from shifting. It goes over the horses neck and straps to either side of the saddle as well as slipping under the chest and attaching to the girth.

Breeches: Special pants; usually soft with padding on the legs for protection and a better grip while riding.

Bridle: A device that goes on the horse's head, to which the bit is attached to aid in steering and controlling the horse.

Canter: A three-beat gait, that when made faster, can become a gallop.

Combination: A series of jumps in a line.

Crop: A small whip that the rider uses to reinforce leg cues; it asks the horse to go forward.

Dapples: Round spots of a lighter color or differences of light on a horse's coat that suggests a healthy coat.

Electrolytes: A sodium based supplement to replace the salt and other essential minerals that are lost through sweating.

Equestrian: One who rides horses.

Gallop: The fastest gait a horse is capable of. It has four beats.

Girth: Goes around the horse's belly to hold the saddle in place.

Green: An inexperienced horse; often young and in need of training.

Groom: A term used when referring to a horse being brushed.

Flatwork: A term used when riding on the flat, with no jumping involved.

Hack: A synonym for trail ride.

Hand: A measuring system for horses where one hand is equal to four inches. A horse's height is measured from the ground to the withers, or base of the neck.

Halter: Can be made of leather or cloth, goes on the horse's head for control while leading.

Hunter circle: A circle made before jumping a course, to prepare the horse for what is to come.

In-and-out: A jumping term where the horse jumps a fence, takes a stride and jumps another obstacle

Join-up: A technique introduced by cowboys to form a bond between the horse and its handler.

Jumping boots: Protective gear placed on the horse's legs, while jumping or galloping.

Liverpool: A large pan of water placed under a jump.

Longe: (Pronounced lunj and sometimes spelled lunge) (noun) A long rope fastened to a horse's head and held by a trainer. (verb) The use of a longe by a handler who stands in the center of a circle and signals the horse to go around him on the rope. (Past tense: longed (lunjd)

Muzzle: A horse's nose.

Oxer: A smaller jump in front, followed by a larger jump with a gap between the two.

Paddock boots: Boots that scarcely come above the ankle; short boots.

Posting: The act when a rider goes up and down with the movement of the horse's legs.

Rail: A term meaning the edge of the arena; also called the track; the pole or plank of a jump.

Saddle: A piece of equipment that goes on the horse's back just behind the neck; it is where the rider sits.

Saddle Pad: A small blanket that goes under the saddle and protects the horse from being rubbed.

Serpentines: Loops made while riding to develop the suppleness and attentiveness of the horse.

Snaffle: A very mild bit that is attached to the bridle and worn in the horse's mouth.

Standard: Support used to hold the rails of a jump; there are two on either side of the poles.

Tack: (noun) Equipment necessary for riding a horse. (verb) To put the tack on the horse.

Tall boots: Boots that end just below the rider's knee. Give grip and protection while riding.

Trot: A bouncy two-beat gait in which the horse's legs move in diagonal pairs. Example, the horse's right fore will move with the left hind.

Untack: To remove the saddle and bridle or other articles placed on the horse for riding.

Vertical: A straight jump that is parallel to the ground.

The Miranda and Starlight six book series
by Janet Muirhead Hill

Middle-grade fiction about the bond between two free-spirited creatures, a girl and a horse. This six book series for readers ages 8-14 tackles contemporary issues in an exciting drama that keeps readers turning the pages.

10-year-old Miranda Stevens lives with her grandparents on their Montana dairy farm while her mother seeks a career in Los Angeles. Miranda finds it hard to fit into a small school where all the other girls in her class are daughters of cattle ranchers and have horses of their own. When Miranda accepts a dare from the class bully, her troubles—and a deep and lasting love for a young stallion—begin.

When asked to make three wishes, Miranda answers, a best friend, a regular family, and a horse of her own. Throughout the six books of this award-winning series, Miranda and Starlight, exhibit courage, loyalty, and trust, as Miranda learns the value of honesty and friendship—and her wishes, one by one, come true in the process.

Grandma and Grandpa and even the old groom, Higgins, offer the impulsive Miranda a solid base of steadfast love and concern. From the strange mismatch of characters, an extended family unit is drawn together with Miranda at its center. Each member learns valuable lessons from the mistakes they make. It is a story of kids coming of age as they meet contemporary issues and, through trial and error, begin to find their own truths.

Fergus, the Soccer-Playing Colt

by Dan A. Peterson

This witty, fast-paced account chronicles the adventures of a palomino colt who was bred to play polo but becomes a soccer goalkeeper, instead. As news of this wonder-colt spreads, he and the two boys who love him, Bobby and Ramon, are taken on a tour of the nation to promote soccer. Hearing of the famous colt, an unscrupulous rodeo stockman and his colorful sidekicks seek to capitalize on the colt's athletic ability. You'll laugh at Rumble and Reiterate as they plan and carry out a horsenapping—and reap the consequences.

Absaroka by Joan Bochmann

In this heartfelt drama of love, war, and the tenacity of the human spirit, young Matt Reed returns from Vietnam to the Wyoming ranch that has been in his family for three generations before him. Matt, who is struggling with the after-effects of war, is confronted with challenges of a changed world and a ranch in jeopardy. His attempts to solve the dilemma, show him the importance of overcoming pride to accept help from ranching neighbors, old friends, the Crow tribe, and even a herd of wild horses.

An Inmate's Daughter by Jan Walker

This middle-grade fiction, set in Tacoma, Washington and at McNeil Island Corrections Center, shows just what it feels like to have a parent in prison. 13-year-old Jenna, who feels ostracized and isolated, struggles to find her identity and her place in society. When she jumps into Puget Sound to rescue a little girl, her mother is furious at her for drawing attention to the island where her dad is a prisoner. Jenna, who wants to be part of the school's multi-racial "in group" finds it hard not to break her mother's don't-tell rule. This engaging story reflects the reality faced by over two million American children with a parent in prison or jail. The children are doing time, too.

Danny's Dragon by Janet Muirhead Hill

Ten-year-old Danny's father went to war in Iraq and was killed in action. Danny struggles with the various stages of grief as he remembers good times with his father. With his vivid imagination, he turns Dragon, the horse his father gave him, into a means of escaping the reality he cannot accept. To add to his grief, financial problems caused by his father's death force Danny, his mother, and sister to leave their Montana ranch. Danny's struggle to understand himself, his family, and the world is compounded when he attends a Denver public school and comes face to face with the "enemy" — a boy from Iraq.

To order, please contact:

Raven Publishing, PO Box 2866, Norris, MT 59745

Phone 866-685-3545   Fax 406-685-3599

www.ravenpublishing.net email: info@ravenpublishing.net